GUY

House of Frazier Book 4

KATHI S. BARTON

This is a work of fiction. Names, characters, places, and incidents are products of the author's imagination or are used fictitiously and are not to be construed as real. Any resemblance to actual events, locations, organizations, or persons, living or dead, is entirely coincidental.

World Castle Publishing, LLC
Pensacola, Florida
Copyright © 2025 Kathi S. Barton
Hardback ISBN: 9798294921767
Paperback ISBN: 9798891264496
eBook ISBN: 9798891264502
First Edition World Castle Publishing, LLC, August 4, 2029
http://www.worldcastlepublishing.com

Licensing Notes

Cover: Cover Designs by Karen
Editor: Karen Fuller

Chapter 1

Guy looked over the list that he was going to take to his brother. He'd looked it over so many times that he could recite it without the paper. What he was doing was avoiding having to talk to him. Guy didn't like people at all. Dead or alive.

"Are you going to go or sit there on your butt all afternoon. I told you that the list was important for the elderly in the pack, didn't I?" Guy would swear that Belinda, Belinda Gross, was as bad as his sisters-in-laws in being pushy, too. The difference was that Belinda was dead and not running around in his business. Not as much as they did anyway.

Ten years ago now, Belinda had been murdered. And her crime had never been solved. So in her free time, something that she told him daily she had a great deal of, she'd been wandering around the town and getting into anyone's business that she wanted to. And thusly, the list that he had. In return for her help, Belinda wanted Guy to contact her stepdaughter so that she'd know there was insurance on her, so that she could collect it. If she didn't do it soon, she'd lose out on the money, and her ungrateful kids would get it.

It wasn't just the elderly in his pack, but the former Alpha, too, that was causing trouble. His name was Lincoln Bates, alpha to the pack that his brother Lica had taken over. He was still profiting off the pack and the things that he'd set up with the school money and pack money, too.

That too had been a disaster in that the teachers—really anyone who worked there—were taking the money that had been earmarked for things such as a new parking lot or new equipment for the kids to play on. None of the programs that Lica had set up were being used, either, like the lunch program and the breakfast for the kids. With the help of Lincoln and that of his wife and four sons, they had it set up under the guise of his retirement to steal from the pack's money and living the life of the rich.

The woman in charge of the ill-gotten gains—another teacher—had stolen enough for brand new cars and trucks, as well as vacation and summer homes. It had been going on for ten years until—thanks to his nieces going there, she was caught. The teacher had told Lica that he should just leave things the way that they were, and she'd take care of it, going so far as to smacking him around a bit to prove her point. To prove *their* point, Brandy, Lica's mate to his alpha, ripped her throat out, decapitating her for all the other wolf teachers to see.

Leaving his new house, one that he'd gotten right before Christmas, was hard on him. Guy liked his solitude and didn't want to hang out with people any more than he had to. He'd had enough at Christmas time, and now he had to do this. Getting to his brother's house, he handed him the list.

"I think since I got hit in the head by the mayor's wife when she was having issues, I can see ghosts. Well, one of them. Her name is Belinda Gross, and she's a tiger. I don't know how she was killed, so don't ask me. But I'm going to help her solve her murder and get her stepdaughter money that was supposed to go to her, too." Lica just stared at him. "Well, do you want to go over the list or not. I have stuff to do and I want to go home."

"Have you always been this rude, or am I just now noticing it?" He told him that he'd forever been rude, and he didn't know why he'd only just noticed it. "Good to know, I guess. What's with the list? Or are you going to snap my head off for that, too?"

"Probably. It's a bunch of shit that's going on with the pack, and what Bates is into concerning the pack. And she said that he's still profiting off the pack's elderly in a big way." He asked how. "Something about social security checks coming to them. He gets a cut from them when he takes them to the bank and cashes them. The other banker, Slaven, would just give him cash for them without question, but now he has to have written permission from the elderly to be able to cash their checks for them. They all signed it so that they could have their money brought to them. Most of them don't have access to a car or anyone to help them with money, so he takes what he wants from them, leaving them with little to no money."

"I guess this has been going on for a while, then." He said that they even think that Bates is still the alpha since they've never seen anyone but him. "Since the school incident, I've been going to different areas of the pack land to check up on things and people. I've really fucked up with this pack, don't you think?" He told him not to ask him unless he wanted an answer. "Well? What do you think?"

"I think you've been taking the word of a monster, and it's coming back to bite you in the ass. But that could just be me." Guy was startled when his brother laughed. "What's so funny?"

"Don't write greeting cards unless you do it for the shock value. What else is on this list?" As they went over each point, Guy was trying not to be mad at his brother for questioning him. He had to know, and that's what he was here for, but he didn't want to be here. "What does this mean right here about the grocery store? That's all it says."

"Gary Larson owns the grocery store. Like the banker, he's only allowing the pack to buy things if they pay him a fifty percent tax on anything they buy. That's why he's been able to add onto the store and have all the windows replaced. He's not a pack member or anything, but that's another thing that Bates is collecting on while retired." He asked him what he'd do. "Kill them all and leave their bodies out for the buzzards."

"Do you have any filter at all?" He shrugged. He told him not to ask if he didn't want an answer. "Look. Could you cut me some slack here? I've been only alpha for about eight months. This sounds like it's been going on for years."

"About that, yeah." Guy looked over the list. "Belinda said that Bates has his hand in everything that goes on with the pack. They've been stealing the wood that you have stored up for the winter months. He has his hand in the food bank, too. The only things that he's not got into, and that's only because it's new, are the underground things you have going on. If he gets his hands in that, there won't be a safe person leaving here ever again."

"That's what I'm afraid of too." He looked over the list. "I don't even know where to begin. I'm guessing I have to do something about Bates first, but I don't even know how to begin with that. Did she have any ideas on how to get his hands out of my business? Other than killing him and leaving him out for the buzzards?" Guy said that was all on him. "Good to know both of you aren't alike. Do you see any other ghosts around here that I should be expecting you to befriend?"

"No, just the one." Guy looked around the house. The Christmas decorations were still up, and the house smelled good. "I have me a house now, too. I'm not saying that I want you to come over and visit or anything, but I bought the one on the hill."

"You were never like this before, Guy. Something more is going on. You might have been blunt, but never just plain rude to people." Guy told him that he just couldn't stand people anymore. "So are you planning to stay up in your house and not bother with any of us? You seemed all right at Christmas."

"I can handle little bits of people. And family is all right for a while. But people aren't at all nice, and I just don't like them." He pointed out that his mate, who was more than likely out there, was going to be a people too. "So long as she doesn't want me to go line dancing with her or some other shit, that'll be fine."

Lica laughed. It seemed to be something that surprised him, but he couldn't tell. Asking him if he needed anything else, when he said no, he didn't right now, Guy gathered up his things and started for the door. Lica saying his name had him pause and wait for something like a blow to his body. Not physically, but all the same.

"Can I get a hug from you?" He turned back and started to hug him when he saw another ghost. Telling his brother about her didn't seem important, so he hugged Lica and made his way home. This shit was getting really annoying, and he was going to have to talk to someone about it. So instead of going home, he made his way to Ayden's home to talk to his daughter, Selma.

The eight-year-old could see ghosts, too. She'd been shot in the head by her father some months ago, and Brandy, with her magic, had saved her from dying. Since then, she'd been able to see ghosts and learned to deal with them. He was going to get with her and see how she handled things. She had to be doing better than he was right now.

Selma and Harley, twin girls who were daughters of Summer and Ayden, greeted him with open arms. For whatever reason, they didn't bother him as much as grown-ups did. They had taken care of him when he'd been hit in the head a few weeks ago, coming out of the storage house.

The mayor's wife, having mental issues of her own, had hit him with a baseball bat hard enough that if it had been a human, they would surely have died.

As it was, he only had a bad concussion. They had made him a sweet card with too much glitter on it and had pampered him. It had been nice right up until it wasn't, and he went home.

"You see more than one or two?" He told Selma that he thought that he'd only seen the one at his house, but there had been one at Lica's home, too. "They usually run in packs. I don't know why, but I only help them one at a time. Is your ghost nice to you? I don't know what I'd do without Harley being around me all the time. Ghosts don't know that she can send them away, but when they get mean with me, she does it. It's kind of funny how silly they can be."

"What do you do to get them out of your life?" She told him that if she helps them, they just go away on their own. Otherwise, she sends them on their way if they get nasty with her. "None of them has gotten nasty with me. Yet."

"They might not ever." She asked him what his ghost wanted from him. After telling her, she nodded. "If you do the list, I don't know what that might do for her, but I'm betting that when you talk to her stepdaughter, she'll be all right to leave. You just have to play that one by ear."

"I will." He thought of something else. "Can your ghosts make lists? I don't know how she was to remember the list she gave me, but I swear now that I think on it, she had a list of her own."

"If they get angry enough, they can touch you, but I've never had one have a list before. But then I'm just a kid and they know that." She smiled at him, and Guy felt it all the way to his heart. "I love you, Uncle Guy. You should come around more often. I know that you don't like people, but we're just kids and you love us."

"I do love you two. Very much." He looked longingly at the door. "I should be going. I have things that need my attention."

"Stay for dinner. I know that mom and dad will love that." He didn't want to stay for dinner, but she'd been helpful to him, and he didn't want to snap at her or her sister. They were great kids. He told her that if it was all right with their parents, he'd stay. Of course, they thought it was a great idea. He felt like he couldn't win around people.

After dinner, which wasn't as bad as it could have been, he made his way to the house. Belinda was either in another part of the house or she'd gone out to nib some more into people's business. The book he started on a week ago was sort of calling to him to write some more, but once he got his computer open, he decided to see if he could find Belinda's stepdaughter. It was easier than he thought it should have been.

He had all the information about her. Not just

her name, but her birthdate and where she'd been living at her last address. According to the things he'd found for her, she'd been living in the same house since her stepmom had been killed. Pulling up the name of the insurance company, wondering why they'd not done very much in the way of contacting her for the policy, he made a call to them. They were still in business, but he'd not realized how late it was, so he didn't leave a message for them to call him back. Next, he tried to call Amber Gross.

~*~

Amber was washing her dishes when her phone rang. Whoever it was, it was more than likely a spam call. She'd been getting them since she'd put the phone back in working order. It had taken her nearly a month of getting the people who called her to realize they weren't calling a doctor's office but her home. Sometimes she still got emergency calls to her home in the middle of the night, looking for Doctor Shipley. She answered it on the second ring.

"My name is Guy Fraizer." She thought that he sounded like she should know him. When she asked him what he wanted, he seemed startled by the question. "I know your mom. Your stepmom, Belinda Gross. She died about ten years ago."

"Is this a joke?" He said that he didn't have a sense of humor, so no, it wasn't a joke. "She's been dead all this time, and you're just now getting around to telling me that you knew her. Why?" He started on something about her murder not being solved, and she cut him off. "You don't think that I know that? I've been working on the case since it's gone cold. What are you calling for now?"

"There is insurance money for you that her kids are going to get if you don't go to the insurance office within the next thirty days and claim it." She asked him again who he was. "I told you. I'm Guy Frazier. Just a friend of your moms."

She wrote down all the information that he had for her mom and decided that he was lying. There was no way that Belinda would have singled her out over her kids. No matter what kind of pieces of shits they were. She asked him how he knew about the insurance money.

"She told me to tell you the truth, but you won't believe me. But she did tell me some things that only she would know about you. The money is right there. You just need to take a copy of your birth certificate and two forms of ID, like I told you." She asked him what he knew. "That when you were ten years old, you wrote in your diary that you wanted to be a big cat like she was, and the other thing is…" He paused for so long that she thought that she'd lost him. "She said that you lost your virginity to a boy by the name of Wintercrest."

The only other persons who knew that were, of course, Jimmy and Belinda. She'd never even written it in her diary. And Jimmy had died not six months after having the worst sex in her life with, and then Belinda five years later. She asked him again where he got the information.

"Look, you're going to go and get the money, right?" She told him she was going to the insurance company first thing in the morning. "Then why do you want to know how I know? I just know, all right? Just get your money and do something great with it. Or don't. I don't care what you do. I'm hanging up now before I say anything else that you might regret."

The phone went dead not a second later, and she put it back in the receiver. Sitting in her kitchen, thinking about what he'd said, she wondered what had prompted him to call her tonight about the insurance money. It had to be something more. Writing down his name and number that had come up on her caller ID, she was going to call him and bother him if it turned out to be a lie. Or thank him if it was true.

She tried to think what this man would gain if she went to the office in the morning and was able to claim the insurance policies. Amber started to ask herself why the kids didn't tell her, and answered her own question. Because they didn't like her. But the more she thought about it, the more she realized that Belinda might have singled her out over her own flesh and blood. They were jerks of the highest order. They'd never treated her right. Not even her dad for as long as he was in the picture.

Her dad had married Belinda when she'd been three. Belinda then had Margaret and Shawn right after the wedding, about a month later. She'd already figured out that they got married because of the kids, but it didn't matter to her. Belinda was as nice a mother as she'd ever had. But the kids were not nice from the moment she'd brought them home from the hospital. The twins had hated her since they were old enough to learn what the feeling was.

Her dad and Belinda had tried to protect her as much as they could. Sometimes, Shawn, even at a young age, would torment her to the point of tears about anything he deemed not perfect. And Amber was far from perfect in his eyes. With her red hair and purple eyes, she was a standout most of the time. Shawn and Margaret were blonds with the bluest eyes she'd ever seen, mostly like her dads but lighter in color.

Getting a shower now that the sun was coming up, she fixed her hair into a nice fat braid at the back of her head, and pulling on her sunglasses, she made her way to the insurance office with her needed identification. She was going to see if the other man was right in saying that she had insurance.

"Oh, Ms. Gross, we've been trying to find you. Your brother and sister said that you were dead, but they didn't have any proof of that. And Mrs. Gross had made it plain that you were to get the money over them. So nice to see you." She said she lived less than a couple of miles from the place. "Did you not see the ads in the newspaper? We put them in there once a week since your mother passed on."

"It doesn't matter now, does it? I'm here, and I'm willing to do what it takes to get the money. I sure could use it." He had her sign off on the identification she'd brought in when he'd made copies of it. Telling her it was for the other two when they came in, inquiring about the money, they could show them that she'd been the one who got it. "Was there a will?"

"There is one. We'll get to reading it as soon as the other two can be gathered up to show up on time. They're not at all prompt." She didn't point out that they had never been as children either. She doubted that it had gotten much better over the years. "Now, the policy has nothing to do with the will, though she did want to make sure you got to hear the will, too. What day would be good for you to do this?"

"Today?" Mr. Brush said that he'd try to get in touch with the kids and see what they could do. "I guess it was in the paper about the will reading, too. You know my brother and sister knew where I lived. They'd stop by a few times a month to harass me about money."

"They have been persistent about the money. I don't know...well, I can guess why they didn't want you to have the insurance. In a few short weeks, without you claiming it, the money would have gone to them. I believe they knew that, too." She told him that she was sure that they did and thought about Guy. "Now, let's get this policy out of the way, and I'll have my assistant try to get in touch with your family."

She wanted to tell him that they weren't her family, but didn't. Again, thinking of Guy, she wondered how he knew her mom. He didn't sound much older than she was, and she was only twenty-five. Her mother had been dead for ten years now, so he would have known her when he was just a kid, just like her.

"Here it is." She looked over the policy and, for the most part, didn't understand what it said. There was a staggering amount of money in the form of a check, so she couldn't get over that. At half a million dollars, it was more money than she'd seen in her lifetime. Maybe two lifetimes. "You just need to sign this form saying that we gave you the check from the insurance policy, and we can move on to other things that she left you. A house for one and money set up to pay the taxes, too. She also had some things that were left from the marriage to your father that she wanted you to have. This is in addition to the will we have to read. She took very good care of you."

She looked over the listing for the house, and she was thrilled that it was the one that she'd lived in with her father before marrying Belinda. It had been a pretty little two-bedroom that had a pool and a pool house in the back. She was as excited about that as she was about the check. And now she was going to have a roof over her head that she didn't have to worry about and money in the bank.

The reading of the will was going to be at two in the afternoon. Shawn and Margaret would be there, but Mr. Brush said to expect them to be late. She knew that without him telling her, and was in too good a mood to care if they showed up or not. There was money for her to get out of the low-paying job that she had and stay in her own home. She didn't even mind that she'd been paying rent on the thing now that she knew that it belonged to her.

Amber knew there was going to be trouble from the other two, but she wasn't going to worry about it now. For some reason, Guy and his call had come to her again, and she wondered if he'd come and rescue her. Silly thoughts like that will get you into trouble, she told herself.

It was nearly three o'clock when Shawn showed up. And almost three forty-five when Margaret decided to roll in. Neither of them acknowledged her, only just to say that they knew she couldn't stay away and plopped — a word that she now understood, seeing the two of them do it — down in one of the chairs to be there for the reading.

The two of them got the house that they'd grown up in, and she was thrilled for them. Having her own home, it was nice to know that they'd not be taking hers. She hoped so anyway. They weren't left any money, and that was all right too. It was Margaret who asked her how much the policy was that she'd gotten from their mom.

"She was my mom too, you know." Margaret scoffed at her and told her that they'd say if she was her mom or not. That must have made better sense in her head because it meant nothing to her when she said it. "It was enough that I don't have to worry about taxes for a while." And that's all she told them.

"I was going to have a fit if you got the bigger house. We wouldn't even all fit in that little one that you grew up in." She said it was perfect for her. "You'd think that, wouldn't you? Well, so long as you don't try to take it from us, I don't care where you live. But that insurance policy needs to be divided up five ways. Shawn and I should get twice as much as you do because they were both our parents."

"No, I don't think so. She left that to me. And I'm going to keep all of it. As I said, it's not all that much, and it will go a long way in keeping me in my house. Besides, I think my dad left you two some money too." She said he did her too. "Well, he was my dad before he was yours, so that makes sense."

After they left with the deed to the house, she decided to wait until they were gone for a little while before venturing out on the streets. She wanted to go and see her home as it was hers now, but was afraid that they'd follow her and do something terrible to it. It would be like them to tear up her home instead of theirs just because they could.

"Ms. Gross, you have a phone call." She said she didn't know who could be calling her as she had a cell phone. "I don't know, but he told me to tell you it was Guy."

"Oh." Going to the phone, she said her name when she picked it up. Guy was talking to someone else, so she waited. She could have sworn that he called someone Belinda, but was sure she just heard that wrong. When he got on the phone with her, finally, she wondered why on earth he could be calling her.

"Shawn and Margaret are planning to ambush you when you go to your place." She asked him how he knew that. "I just do, all right? They want the money from the check. They really couldn't care less if it's ten dollars or ten million, they feel that you owe it to them for getting it, and they didn't."

"You have to tell me how you know this and how you know my mom. She's been gone for a while, and since I'm sure you didn't know her as a kid, you have to tell me." He said she'd not believe him. "Mister, I'm pretty open-minded and will believe most anything. Even if you were to tell me that she's a ghost and she's haunting you."

He didn't say a word. His end of the conversation was so quiet that she had to look at the phone to see if she was connected. Asking him if he was still there, he told her that he was and that he did see her as a ghost.

"I don't believe you." He laughed. It was a bitter laugh, too, that hurt her heart to hear it. "Who would believe you can see ghosts. No one does."

"My niece does, and she helps them. Several weeks ago, I was hit in the head and nearly killed by a human. I'm a shifter wolf. I don't suppose you believe in those either, do you?" She said she knew some shifters. "So you'll believe a man turns into a wolf, but not one that can see your dead mother. If it helps you at all, I'm going to help solve her murder, too. I believe I can do it."

"They did it. Just like they killed my dad, Shawn

and Margaret did it. I don't know how, and I have no proof, but as sure as I'm sitting here, they killed them both off." He told her he was sorry. "Not as sorry as they'll be when I get it figured out."

"I can help you." She asked him why he'd do that. "As I said, your mother is a friend of mine now, and she's been keeping me company."

"Because you can see her ghost." It wasn't a question, but he answered it anyway. "I don't want to believe you, but I feel that you're telling me the truth. I mean, why would you lie to me about seeing her? You have nothing to gain."

"You have nothing I want either. Not your money nor your house. I have that and a house." He was sort of rude, and she asked him what that was about. "I don't like people. They're rude most of the time and don't understand when someone is rude back to them. Hang on a minute. Your mom is going to see if they're still at your home. By the way, she said not to go to the bank either. They'll catch you there for sure. That's a wonderful idea. Belinda said to use some of the money you got for a security system. Don't get yourself dead before you can enjoy your home."

Yes, he was a rude shit.

Chapter 2

Belinda didn't like that the kids were still hanging out at Amber's place. They were in their new car, she wondered how they could afford that—and watching the house while they got food delivered to them. They were a pair, the two of them.

She thought about how Amber said that they'd killed her. She didn't know how, but she thought that they had. They had killed their father, too, she'd said. Thinking about the night that she'd been killed, she no more knew what had killed her than what she had explained to Guy.

Coming out of the car when it had been nasty cold, Belinda had thought that she'd fallen. Hit her head on the cold ground and died. But the police report said that it was more than likely a baseball bat that had hit her, and the blunt force trauma had busted her head wide open, and she had bled out. Guy had gotten all kinds of paperwork from the police, but none of it pointed to a murder. He was also writing about her death.

Guy had been writing books since he was

twelve years old. He had all kinds of pieces of paper in a box where he had kept all his ideas for his first book. His family didn't know that he wrote, and he didn't want them to know, but she thought it was neat how he'd just sit down at the computer and write and write for days without stopping. Then he'd get up, eat something, and go back at it. She wouldn't tell him this, of course, but she thought it was wonderful how he did it. Just typing whatever he wanted to the paper and going on to the story. There was also the way he was filling out the house that they shared.

It wasn't small, the house. It had five bedrooms, six and a half bathrooms, as well as a media room— the one he used for his office, as well as a living room, den, dining room, and the nicest kitchen that she'd ever been in. There were other rooms, too, ones that she had no name for, but he would get a few boxes in, put together whatever was in them, and then put it in a room. She liked, too, that he broke down his boxes so they weren't a mess around the house. Guy also kept a neat house. Never anything out of place or in the way.

"This report here says that you were robbed, too. The store you were in said that you paid cash for your groceries and had a good deal left over. But your wallet was empty, as were your pockets." He looked at her when she came into the room. It still startled her when someone would look directly at her these days.

"Do you remember going into the store at all? You said you were getting out of the car to go in, but according to this, you'd already been in there."

"I think I was going back in. I seem to remember not having any ice cream and wanting to go back in and get it. It used to be my one treat I'd give myself." She asked him the name of the grocery store. He told her. "I remember that now. It's been so very long that I'd forgotten that. Mr. Smithies Grocery had just about anything you'd want for being a small place."

She could tell that he didn't care. Guy would be stubborn about things and rude the rest of the time. She thought that he was lonely rather than just rude, but that was just her. He wasn't just nasty to her but to anyone who came by. But for the little girls that she'd seen. Selma and Harley.

Selma could see ghosts because she'd been shot in the head by her father. It wasn't an accident like she thought, but he'd shot her on purpose. Killing her because her momma loved her was a sorry excuse. Harley had been shot, too, but not as life-threateningly as Selma had been. She'd been able to see ghosts since then. Belinda worried about her at first, dealing with the dead, but Harley was her protector, and that made them a good team in working together. They were beautiful, too, just like their father.

All the Frazier men were beautiful. She supposed

they'd be called handsome, but she thought that the way they looked was just too beautiful to ignore. Their dark curly hair and their strong muscles made them eye candy too, she'd thought that she heard them called. Whatever they were, she'd loved to have been around when they were turning into men instead of children when she'd been old enough to date them.

Guy, unlike his brothers, wasn't as outgoing. He would sit in his house all day at the computer and write. They loved to get out and do things. It wasn't as if he never left the house; he did on occasion, but for the most part, he'd write all day or tinker around the house on one of his many household projects.

"You never answered me about your husband. Did you want me to see what I can find out about his death? Do you want me to get a death certificate too?" She said that she'd never thought of him being murdered, but now that it was out there, she wanted to see. "What are the details surrounding his death? Do you know?"

"He was shot during a robbery. Wrong place, wrong time the police had said." He asked her if she believed them. "I'm not sure now. I mean, can a twelve-year-old kill someone and not get caught? That's how old the twins would have been when he was killed. The robber was killed on site. He didn't get very far because someone with a gun killed him, too."

"I'll see what I can find." She thanked him. "I have to go out tomorrow in the morning. I'm going to go and see Amber and help her get some security cameras around her house. She's not been back there since she got it from you, and I can tell that she really wants to go there."

"Would you mind if I went with you? If I have something to say to her, you can tell her." He told her no. "Well, I'll just pester you until you do, then. I know how much you hate my singing now, and I'll do that."

"Why don't you find another house? This one is mine." She told him again that she was there first. "I actually paid for it, and all you did was squat in it."

"I was here first. You find yourself another place. I told you I'd help you. There are any number of houses in the little town that you could live in." She didn't want him to leave, not really. He'd been making the place cozy and warm with his being there. "Besides, where are you going to find yourself another roommate that doesn't cause you trouble like I don't?"

"You cause trouble just by being around. I have better things to do other than to cater to your needs, you know." She thanked him again. "I'm going outside. The mail has run."

Something else she knew about him that none of his family did was that he wrote first of all. Secondly, he did it under a false name. Guy wrote murder mysteries and was really good at it. While she'd not read one herself, she'd read the reviews on the back of the book and was quite impressed. And no matter how much she pestered him, he still wouldn't read it to her so that she could have an idea of the man she was living with. Even if she was dead.

When he left, trudging in the snow banks on his way to town, she wondered what had happened to him that made him so bitter. She'd figured out that it wasn't his brothers. They were all as nice as he was rude. But something had made him like the man that he was, and like her murder, she wanted to get to the bottom of it.

She knew about his parents. You couldn't be dead or alive in this little town without hearing how they treated their kids. She'd also heard that the mother of these fine men had killed their daddy and tried to blame it on them. The police officer, whose name she couldn't remember, had stood up for the boys and had basically adopted them into his own home with his wife to raise them after the mother was put in prison. Maybe they had something to do with him being the way that he was. Or maybe some woman hurt him. He didn't like humans, which she didn't blame him for. Humans were an odd sort of people. But someone had hurt him, and she wanted to know why so that she could perhaps fix him for someone.

She looked in on her treasures, things that she'd been able to pick up from others that she'd liked. Some of it was trash, a set of keys that she'd taken from a house so that the man couldn't drive with his kids in the car while he was drunk. A letter that had come in the mail for a person who would have been hurt had they read it. She'd seen the person writing the nasty letter and had to wait at the house for it to come.

There were also treasures, too. Some lovely silverware—which reminded her of the people that were related to Guy and their underground help system to get people out of abusive relationships. Another ghost had wanted to use his treasures too to help with the railroad, but most of his was stolen, and they were afraid that it would come back on them. Just as she was going to go and look for other things to put away from humans to use, she saw a woman walking down the street with her twins behind her.

It was Amber; she just knew it was. And if she didn't get any help, she was going to get hurt by the kids. Damn it all to hell and back. She needed to get some help. It was then that someone knocked on the door to their home. Looking at the couple standing there, she wondered how she could get them to help her daughter.

Finding Guy was easy. He only went to two places around, if you didn't count his brother's home;

it was the bank and the post office. Finding him, she told him to call his brother and tell them to find Amber. She was in trouble again. Instead of doing what she wanted, he asked her where she was.

"Just outside the bank." He took off toward the bank a little faster than she thought he could move and intercepted her before Shawn did. She didn't know where Margaret was, but she'd be willing to bet that she wasn't that far behind him. Amber was safe inside the bank when the other one walked by. "She needs to be more aware of what's going on around her. Can you tell her that?"

He did, but it must have triggered something in her head about him because she asked if he was Guy Fraizer. He looked like he wasn't going to answer her, but he did finally, and Amber hugged him.

"Don't get all mushy around me." Guy peeled Amber off him and took several steps back. "Your mother is here. She's the one who warned me about your family. I'm glad that I was able to keep you from getting your head bashed in."

"Yes. I knew it had to be you. You're the rudest man I've ever talked to. Can she hear me if I just talk to her?" He told her daughter how it worked with her being able to hear her talking. "Good. And you'll tell me what she says? I have some questions to ask you both. Why are you looking at me like that?"

"Mates. We're mates. Damn it." Belinda laughed. It did her heart good to know that Amber would be safe from now on because of her being with Guy, but she also thought it was funny that he'd found his mate today, and it was her little girl. "I don't want a mate, especially a human one."

"Well, isn't that just too bad for you? Me too if you think you're going to be rude to me for the rest of our lives. In the event you're wondering, you're not." She looked around and smiled. "Tell me where Belinda is so that I can pretend to hug her. And don't be rude when you tell me what she's saying to me."

"Do you think we can do this later? Your sister is looking for you, and now I'm going to have to make sure that you're all right with her around." She glared at him, and Belinda laughed again. "Laugh it up, and I'll pretend like I don't hear you when you want to have a talk with her. I mean it. I will."

"Let's go back to your house. They'd never think to look for her there." He begrudgingly agreed. Belinda was more determined than ever to find out what had happened to him to make him the man that he was. If he was going to be around her daughter all the time, she wanted answers and soon. "Be nice to her. I know you can, I've seen you being nice to those little girls."

He growled low in his throat, and she laughed again. Not as loudly as before, he was making sure that

Amber got out of the bank safely. She'd just have to dig around for something—perhaps one of his brothers might know something. She'd figure out a way to get them to tell her soon.

Belinda didn't mind the cold. She was dead after all, but she could tell that it was too much for Amber. Not only did she seem to be freezing, but she didn't have the right boots on or coat. Before she could think of something to do for her, Guy took off his coat and put it on her shoulders. Amber didn't fight him either, telling him thanks through chattering teeth.

It took them twenty minutes to get back to the house on the hill. Instead of taking his coat back, Guy got several of the new little quilts that were on the back of the couch and wrapped Amber up in them. While doing that, he also turned on the gas fireplace and got a roaring fire in it. After dragging her to the fireplace, he went to make her some hot cocoa. This was a new Guy and she liked him.

After two cups of hot cocoa and thirty more minutes in front of the fireplace, Amber looked as if she was thawing out. Guy asked her why she wasn't dressed better, and she thought that Amber was going to hit him. Instead, she simply turned in the chair so she didn't have to look at him.

"I've not been able to cash the check yet. So I don't have the money for a new coat and boots. I was hoping to get them while they're on sale, but I don't have the money. Again, I can't cash my check." He told her that he'd buy them. "No, you won't. You're already mean to me, and I don't want to be beholden to you any more than I have to. You're a mean person and a rude bastard."

"I'm sorry, but when I see a grown woman in a heavy sweater and not a coat, I do wonder what's going on. You should have said something to me. I would have gotten you whatever you wanted or taken the car to the bank to get you." She huffed at him. "That's really mature. Did you miss your nap by any chance?"

When she stood up, dropping the blankets and coat off of her, Belinda took a step back. Even her tiger was a little scared at the face that was looking at Guy. When Amber announced that she was leaving, he stood up as well and blocked the doorway.

"Don't be stupid. You'll catch your death." She told him it was better than putting up with him. "I'm sorry. I'll try to tone it down a bit, but I'm worried that you might have caught something out there, and I don't want you sick." Amber glared at him some more. "I'm not used to having people around me that I should be nice to. The others just take it. They might bust my chops about being so rude, but they take it from me."

"Perhaps you should be nice to everyone. Whoever shit in your oats has made you this way, and it's too much for anyone." She stayed nearer to the fire, and Belinda was glad for that. "I'm betting there is a lynch mob after you about now. And for as rude as you've been to me, I'd help them."

"I said I was sorry. What else do you want me to do? Give you my blood?" She said she wanted him to be nice; was that so hard? "It is, actually. I'm rude to everyone; it's not just you. Christ, this is why I didn't want to have a mate. Now I not only have to be nice, but I have to put up with you being a human. It's not your fault, I know, but something that I have to work on."

"Why? Why are you such a rude person when being nice is so much easier?" He told her that it was none of her business. "Of course it is, I'm your mate from now on, and that's the way it should be. No secrets between us at all. So tell me what has made you like you are so that I can take care of them. It had to be a woman, that's all I can think about."

"It was a woman, damn it."

~*~

Guy didn't want to have to tell anyone how he'd been hurt. It still was as fresh a hurt today as it had been several years ago when he'd been just sixteen. Not even his brothers knew about the woman who had treated him so callously. Now he was trapped into telling his mate what had happened so that he could be humiliated once again.

"Her name isn't important. But she was older than me and had asked me out." He looked at the fireplace that had been keeping the two of them warm for the past hour before he spoke again. He couldn't even look at Amber for fear of what would be on her face. "I'd just been sixteen and we were no longer living with our parents. The Wilkins had taken us in when the courts allowed them to raise us. They were good people and did a good job of raising us up to be good people, too."

He thought about how the couple had helped them buy the farm that Lica had been running for them and how they'd barely made ends meet. But after meeting Brandy, she'd made sure they were wealthy enough to buy their own homes, and it had worked out very well for them all. Guy looked at Amber, then Belinda.

"She kept pestering me to go out with her. She was at least twenty-five, and I had no idea at sixteen why she would date someone like me. Just a kid. Of course, I didn't look all that much like just a kid at the time. I'd matured early and had a beard by then. But she kept at me until I said yes." Amber asked her name and if she still lived in town. "Yes, and no, I'm not going to tell you her name. Suffice it to say, she no longer bothers my family with her hurtful ways."

"But she is still hurting you." He knew that on some level as well, but didn't mention her name. Guy did, however, go on with his story about her and why he was so bitter about people. "She's human. You can tell me that, right? She's a human."

"Yes, she's human." He thought about the date and knew that it was going to come off with him sounding like the fool in all of this. "She only wanted to go out with me so that I'd shift and fuck her." There he'd said it.

"And? There has to be more to it than that. Or did you mean as your wolf?" He nodded. "I see. I don't know what I would have done either. But that doesn't seem like enough for you to be so bitter about. There's more to it than just that."

"She wanted to film us fucking." Amber told him to stop beating around the bush and to tell her what had happened. "She wanted us to have sex, me as my wolf. But before that, she convinced me to kill her husband because he was so mean to her. Come to find out, she likes her sex rough, and she had lovers who would beat her during sex. She thought because I was sixteen and having sex with her, she could convince me to kill off her husband and go to prison for it."

"How did you get out of it? I'm sure that you didn't kill her husband, and it's doubtful to me that you had sex with her as your wolf, too." He just stared at Amber. "I've only known you for like a couple of hours, but I wouldn't ever doubt that you'd turn her in over being caught up in a murder for sex scheme."

"Mr. Wilkins said the same thing when I told him. He told me that I was a good man who had been hurt by her and that I shouldn't allow it to get into my head like she'd done." He sat down in the chair next to the fireplace. "She told anyone that would stop by to see her that I'd raped her as my wolf and that I had come up with the plan to kill her husband. He did end up getting killed, but by her, not me. But she put so much blame on me that I was arrested after a while." She asked if his brothers had known about what had happened. "No. They…I didn't have a great deal to do with them while I was growing up, for one reason or another. Mostly, I was working as much as I could to make ends meet, or I was hiding someplace writing. Mostly the writing part. I published my first book when I was eighteen, so I'd been busy."

"So this woman, who will forever be known as 'bitch,' pesters you to the point you finally give in to her and go out. You then find out that she wants to have sex with your wolf while you no doubt nip and scratch at her so that she can get off. She wants you to kill her husband, because she believes you're either too immature or too stupid to think beyond your dick with any kind of sense that you'll just blindly do what she asks of you because to her, you'll be too infatuated with her to do anything but what she says." Amber scoffed. "I hope she got life without parole for this stunt. And for the record, I might have sworn off humans, too. Especially if someone treated me that way."

Guy couldn't help it. He burst out laughing. He didn't know what he had expected, but full acceptance of what had happened wasn't even close to anything he'd thought. The more he thought about what she had said, the more he laughed. It was something that he'd not done in longer than he could remember, and that sort of made him sad.

"The police believed me because they knew my brothers." Amber looked ready to do battle for him. Or to him, he couldn't tell which. "I worked with the police by wearing a wire, and that's when I figured out that she only wanted to have me go to prison. I guess as a young kid, I didn't want to think that she was using me. I should have spoken to my brothers, but by then it was too late."

"How did they not know?" He told Belinda that he had no idea, but they were also wrapped up in the things to do with their parents. His dad had only just been killed, and their mom was saying that they'd done it, killed him, and was trying to blame it on them. "Okay, I can see that. They were so wrapped up in what was going on in their own life that they might not have noticed what was—I hope you plan on telling them. I don't doubt that she hurt you, Guy, but you have such a wonderful family that I can't believe that they wouldn't have helped you a great deal with your issue as well."

"My father was human, too, remember? And our mom was half human. The very fact that it turned out that all of us were able to shift is a miracle. Also, we didn't tell our parents at all that we could shift. They would have used us as our wolves to get us into trouble that would have cost us our lives. Either going to prison or just getting killed. We didn't tell anyone but the Wilkins, and they would have died before telling anyone." Amber said she heard about his parents. "They weren't the best of the lot, but I'm to understand from people, humans again, that they shaped us into what we are. What I wouldn't give for one of them to have lived the nightmare that we lived with them. Then they'd know we didn't get shaped more like we got beaten into submission to be the people that we became."

"I'm so sorry that you had to go through all of that alone, Guy. I truly am." He'd been told that all his life that people were sorry for his lot in life, but he felt like Amber had meant it. He nodded to her, the lump in his throat stuck there because of his emotional turmoil that he was going through. "I bet once you tell

your brothers what happened to you, they'll give you
the best hugs. I've noticed that, that your family gives
a lot of hugs. Oh, to have one of them when I'm down
and out. Which seems to happen to me a great deal of
late with my brother and sister around, trying to hurt
me."

"Right. About them. I'll make sure they
understand that you're no longer a target for them.
Then if that doesn't work, which I see no reason to think
that it will, I'll have to show them that I mean business
when they step out of line." She asked him why he'd
do that. "You're my mate, and I want to make sure that
nothing happens to you. I don't know that I'll ever get
over being rude to those around me, but for you, I'll
try my best. I swear to you on the heart of Mrs. Wilkins
that I'll keep you as safe as I can, as will my family,
from now on. I just have to make the time to tell them."

"Don't you have that mind melt thing?" Again,
he laughed, not sure why he thought that was funny.
"You should tell them now so that when you take me
home, they'll know if I am in trouble that I'm someone
they should be helping." He asked her what she meant.
"I don't know why I put it like that. Your brothers, even
you, help anyone who needs it, including my mom.
When I think of the things that had to line up to make
sure we were together, it boggles the mind, don't you
think? You got hit in the head, which made it so that

you could see ghosts. Belinda might not have been able to get me contacted in time if you hadn't purchased this house. Then you wouldn't have figured out I was your mate until you had to save me. Just the little things that work through the daily life of us has made me think that we were fated to be together. Isn't that what you think too? That the fates put us together?"

"It's either the fates that put us together or someone who has a dark sense of humor put us together." He didn't want to ask her which she believed in. He was actually afraid of the answer.

He knew that he'd been dumping on others more than he needed to. Things had worked out in a strange way for him to have met her. And not that he was with her as her mate, he wanted to do better than he'd been doing lately. When she asked him if he'd take her home, he suggested that she stay here until the cameras were up. She agreed too readily. And for some reason, he was happy for that. Guy didn't get to be happy about too many things, but this was one of them. He was a happy man right now, and it had been so long that he had completely forgotten about how it felt to be that way again.

Chapter 3

"I don't understand." Shawn was sick of his sister never seeming to understand what he'd say to her. It was getting on his last nerve to have to explain things to her like she was five years old when she was as old as he was. "What does her having cameras all around her home have to do with us trying to get into her house? It's not like she's going to tell the police anything. I can't believe that she's gone this long without telling on us now. She's stupid or something."

"She's putting the cameras in so that she'll have proof that we've been trying to get into her home. And there are locks on the windows that will sound an alarm when someone tampers with them." The look on her face made him want to bash her skull in. "She'll have proof that it's us, not just her telling the police. Now, when they come and ask us about it, they'll have the proof they need to have us arrested. And she did too tell on us before. It's just that she never had anything that she could prove that we'd been tearing up her home."

"What's that have to do with us?" Growling at

her, he just walked away. It was getting harder and harder to want to be in the same room as she was, and he didn't like that feeling. They were twins and were supposed to be on the same page about everything. "I've been watching the bank like you told me, and she's not been there but the one time with that big man. You said you didn't want to be around her when she had someone in her corner."

"No, because she might well have told him that we're hurting her and that would be the end of our little bit of fun." Margaret started to ask him another question, but he cut her off. "It just will, that's all. I'm not going to tell you why again."

"All right, but I know who the big guy was. That's funny. Because the big guy's name is Guy. Get it? His name is Guy and he's the guy." He rolled his eyes at her, then asked what his last name was. "Fraizer. Didn't you have some trouble with one of the Fraizer boys when you were in high school? Something about you saying that he cheated on a test? That didn't work out well for you, if I remember. The school made you both retake the test, and you still flunked it. Didn't he ace the test the second time around?"

"Just shut up about the Fraizer men." He had to think about what it was he had heard about them lately that made him think that he didn't want to fuck with them at all. Then he remembered. "They're dogs, the lot of them." She asked him what he meant, of course. "They can be dogs or something when they get pissed off. Tear your throat right out of you if they get pissed off enough, from what I heard."

He believed it too. Once, when he'd been about ten years old, he'd seen his mom shift into a large tiger. She'd been bigger than the ones he'd seen in the zoo, not the week before, and was terrified of them. Margaret was going on about how their mom was a tiger and she'd never do that. He knew better. He'd seen her in action when someone tried to take one of them from her while out shopping.

"Besides, Mom is gone, thank goodness. I can't believe that we got away with that twice in our lifetimes." He wanted to pretend that he didn't know what she was talking about, but didn't want to get into it with her again. He walked into the kitchen to have some time to think. There was a great deal for him to think about, too.

They'd missed out on the insurance money because someone had called Amber and let her know about it. No matter how many times they tried to convince the policyholders that Amber was as dead as their parents, they wouldn't believe it without a death certificate. Not only that, but when they put the ad in the paper for her to be notified, they'd have to go to all the trouble of stealing her newspapers for the time the ad was being run. It was a lot of work, and if she'd just not known about it for one more month, they would have gotten the money instead of her. As it was now, all they got was their childhood home and nothing more. There was very little money left over from what their father had left them, and Belinda leaving them the house didn't mean as much if there was no way they could live in it for free. Taxes were due again, and they just didn't have the money without the policy. Margaret followed him into the kitchen.

"I'm hungry." So was he, but it did very little good because no one would bring them food anymore. Not even the dumbest of places like pizza. Though he was surely sick of pizza, it would have filled the void about right now. "What do you say you write another check to the bank and they cash it and we have ourselves some feast someplace? You have plenty of checks left."

Another thing that he couldn't make her understand was that just because there were checks that could be written, if there was no money to cover them, then you were more broke than before because of the bounced check fees. She either didn't want to understand or couldn't, but again, it got on his nerves. This time, he didn't even bother with trying to explain.

"We're going to have to sell some more stuff around here." They'd about sold everything that was in the house, from their dining room table and chairs to the pocket watch that his father had left him. Why? No one knew why, he had a cell phone and didn't need a watch that fit in your pockets. He was forever forgetting about it anyway. "How many more pocket watches do we have?"

"Four. And one that I got from mom when she was killed." She could remember stuff like that, but nothing important. "You know, we should have gotten the policy because we had to go through all the trouble of killing her. The least she could have done was leave us some of the money that Dad had left her. And what about the money from Dad's death? What happened to all of it?"

"We spent it poorly and now it's all gone." That was the truth. The first thing they'd got with the money was a new car each. Then they'd splurged on a cruise. And boy did they splurge on it. When they got back, there were taxes to pay, and they were nearly broke by the end of the first month. Two million dollars didn't go as far as they thought it should have. "We should have put some of it to better use than to just spend it like we did. But it was fun."

"Yeah, it was a blast." Margaret sat down at the kitchen table, a table that he'd never eaten at in his entire life. That's what the dining room was for. "We should go on another cruise. We can not spend as much as we did the first time, but just enough to have some fun."

"We don't have enough checks to cover that." He wasn't going to explain that having checks didn't mean you had money again, so he changed the subject. "Tomorrow we'll go and talk to Amber and see how much she's going to give us of the money. Like we've been saying, they were more our parents than they were to her. She just had her dad, and we had them both. And why is Mom even leaving her any money in the first place? We're her kids."

Going up to his room, he was glad that he'd forbidden her from coming to it. She wasn't allowed to knock on his door unless it was an emergency. And the house had better be on fire if she was going to disturb him. Laying out on his bed, the thought of all the things that he wished he'd known before. Like, millions of dollars wasn't all that much in the long term of things, and that spending it like they had would net them nothing. They had nothing to show for the trip. They'd not purchased any souvenirs, nor had they taken all that many pictures. Wasted money, he thought, and now they didn't even have the cars.

Last month, they'd had to sell the cars so that they could afford to have their bills paid. It sucked that there wasn't anyone around who could have paid them for them. When their mom was alive, she always made sure that the power was on and that they had cable and internet. Now they only had internet because having all the channels was much too expensive right now. He knew what Mom would have said about that. She would have told them to get a job again. That was why they'd killed her in the first place, because she was ragging on them to get one so that she would not have to pay for everything that they needed as adults.

"Being an adult sucks." As a teenager, he'd counted the days until he could be an adult. To be able to do what he wanted because he was old enough in the eyes of the law to make his own decisions. But right off the bat, he'd made the wrong decision about some things and had nearly ended up in jail. Then he realized that he had to be the adult for Margaret, too, or they'd be in worse trouble than they were now. Shawn looked over at the desk that had all the final notices on it for their household. Some of them were behind as much as three months, and he saw no way to pay them.

He supposed that he could pay them like Margaret said, just write them checks, and that would be the end of it. Not really, but that wouldn't work anyway; they no longer took his checks for bills because they bounced higher than he could jump.

At midnight, he got up and crept to the front door. He knew that Margaret would have gone to bed by nine-thirty. She was a creature of habit, and since they'd been little, that was their bedtime, and she would adhere to it. Going out into the cold of the night, he nearly went back inside as the wind picked up some of the snow and blew it onto him. But he had a job to do, and he needed to do it now.

He didn't have a car to drive, so he walked the four miles to Amber's home. Even in the darkened night, with all the snow surrounding it, the place looked good. She had planted some flowers in the spring that made him think that he'd love to have someone do that for their place. However, he only scoffed at the idea with his sister so she'd not think he'd gone soft in the head over a bunch of flowers that perked up the place better than their new car had done for their home.

Staying across the street from the place, he looked at the footprints in the snow and saw that there had been a lot of walking around her place to get the cameras put in. He could see the green lights making it known that the house was more secure than not. Shawn wanted to go across the street and rip them from the place, but he knew that would bring the police. The sign right there in the front made it clear to anyone going by that it would happen if tampered with. He was so depressed about it that he wanted to go home and go to bed and not get up. Things with Amber were getting more complicated daily, and he didn't care for it.

"I'm so superior to her that it's laughable that I'm in the situation that I'm in now." It really wasn't laughable, but it did make him want to cry. "She should be begging me to take the money from her rather than us having to go around stealing from her."

He didn't care for stealing at all. Oh, it had been fun at first. To take the things that she'd had simply because they could. But as things went on, the broker they became, it was necessary for them to survive all these years. Her having a job that paid her something was the only reason they would have any food for that night or not.

Some people would say that he needed to get a job. Well, he didn't think he'd ever be that poor that he would need to find himself some employment. It was beneath him to have a job, and he didn't want anyone telling him what to do daily, either. If he were to be found working at some menial job, it was because it was preferable to eating from a dumpster. And that was something that he'd never do in his life. There was movement at the house that drew his attention to the place.

"Shawn Gross." He said his name like it was the awful way of spelling their name. He and Margaret pronounced it like Goss without the 'r'. Shawn told the man that. "I don't care if your name is douche canoe, what are you doing around my future wife's home?"

"Future wife? Oh, I see. She gets a little money, and suddenly you want to marry her." He knew that wasn't true as soon as he said it. The Fraziers had money, and by looking at the man, he could tell that's who he was. "What do you want with a woman like that when you can buy anyone you want. Hell, I'll sell you my sister if that's what you want."

"Make up your mind. Am I broke or rich? I can't be both. But whatever the reason that you're talking about, she is going to be my wife soon. And right now, if you don't back off from harassing her, I'm going to make you regret ever being born." He sort of felt like that daily. "I can read your mind, Shawn. Why would you continue to steal from her when you feel bad about it?"

"I never said that I felt bad about stealing from her. But there are days when I feel like being born to this time isn't what I would have wanted." He had no idea why he was telling the man this, but it felt right. "We were stupid with our money, and now we're broke. How about you give us a few million and I'll leave Amber alone."

"I don't think so." Of course not. Why would he help them? "When I marry her, and it will be sooner rather than later, you'll be my half-brother-in-law. Or something like that. I'm hoping that we can get along better than we're seemingly getting along now."

"You mean that I stop taking from her. I don't think that's going to happen. Not unless you can convince her to hand over her insurance from my mom. Mom wasn't anything to Amber, yet she got all the money."

"You got the bigger house and more money than she did when her own father died. Or did she? I can't imagine that he'd leave his first little girl out in the cold like he did. He seemed like a good man." Shawn snorted and said that he was a sap. "Is that why you killed him? Because he was a sap? Or did you have other reasons for being upset with him? Your mom, too. I know you killed her as well."

"You have no idea what you're talking about." Guy told him what he knew about the death of their mother. "You don't—where are you getting that information? You're just making up about how she was headed into the store instead of out. You don't know anything about it."

"I know that she wanted some ice cream that she'd forgotten to get, and you and your sister came up behind her and hit her with a baseball bat. How hard was it for you to swing it in the icy cold parking lot when you were just kids? I'm thinking you would have had to have some powerful feelings for you to have swung it that hard. Did she piss you off before leaving?"

"She was forever pissing me off. Did you know that she wanted me to get a job in the summer months we were off from school? Why should I have to work when Dad was making all kinds of money?" He didn't say anything. "You should get your facts right before you go spouting off shit you have no idea about."

"You argued with her that day. Telling her that you weren't going to work unless she did. She told you that she had a hard enough job just raising the three of you." That stunned him to silence. But not Guy. "She slapped you, too. Told you that you were going to have respect for her in her home."

"No." Shawn was sure that he couldn't hear him, as it was just a whispered sound. But he'd forgotten he was a shifter and knew that they could hear better than most. "You couldn't know those things. No one knows what happened that day but she and I."

"I'm talking to her right now, Shawn. Do you want to know what else she has to say? She said that you and your sister were brats from the time she brought you home from the hospital and that your dad gave in to you whenever you went to him. But that didn't last forever, did it? He started listening to Belinda after you got into trouble at school when you accused my brother of cheating off of you. That didn't work out so well for you either, did it?"

"You shut your mouth. I told you that you don't

know what you're talking about. Shut up before I come after you." The tightening of the air around him was all the warning that he got before he was shoved into the snowy embankment with a giant dog on his chest. The claws of the thing were digging deeply into his chest, and he cried out with the pain. "Get off me, you stupid mutt. I'm going to sue your ass for this. I swear it."

The snarl had his dick shrink and curl around his ass. It wasn't a pleasant feeling, but he knew that it could have been worse. When the thing nipped at his hand that he was using to push him off with, then there was the lick to his face.

~*~

Guy wanted to rip out his throat and be done with him. But Belinda was begging him to back off and not kill him. What she said was that he wasn't worth it to go to prison for killing him. But he did have a connection with him now, and he planned to use it to do everything he could to make him regret pissing him off.

"What will Amber say when you turn up at the house naked as the day you were born?" For some reason, they had a good connection too, and he told Belinda that he'd be clothed because of him being her mate. "I wish tigers had that. It would have been nice to have had a few times when I was in the yard with their father."

"I don't want to know, thanks." She laughed

and told him that Amber wanted him to come home. "I suppose you told her that I was with her brother, too."

"No, I can't tell her anything. It's sort of my fault that you had to shift, and I'll take full blame for that. Oh, how I wish I had been able to shift as a ghost. That's something that I miss a great deal. I'm glad that the other two were never able to shift. I think it saved a lot of people's lives by them not being able to shift into a tiger." She looked around, wondering why she was even out here. "Let him go, and let's get back home. I've had enough memories...do you suppose that if you were able to call to my husband, he'd remember who killed him and why? I know that the robber killed him, but...I guess that's who we should be calling back. To see if he remembers the kids from the ones who hired him. It would be something that we can look into when you let him go and come back with me."

Guy backed away from Shawn, but not before marking him again. The man deserved whatever would come to him, and he hoped that his luck had finally run out. To think that he and his sister had killed both their parents made him sort of sick. Never once in all their life did the six of them ever think about killing their parents. Not that they didn't try to kill them whenever the chance came around.

Shifting back to himself, he wished that he'd thought of pissing on Shawn while he'd been his wolf.

Making his way back to the house, he got into his car and decided that he'd had enough playing around for one night. He wanted to go home and talk to Amber more. And try his best not to piss her off again. But she surely was beautiful when she got upset.

"You really going to talk to your brothers about the two of them? I'd hate for someone to get hurt because you don't like people." He said he'd contact them all in the morning and let them know that Amber had found him and that her family was sniffing around, trying to get killed. "That's about the way that it is, too. They're going to keep fucking with the wrong man until they get themselves killed. Especially Shawn. He's ten kinds of stubborn."

"I have a connection with him now, so he won't be able to sneak up on me without me knowing. I just have to establish one with Amber so I can talk to her too." She thought that was a good idea as well. "I have them on occasion. Good ideas, I mean."

"If you had too many of them, people would label you a smart ass, and then where would you be?" He said he was trying to be nice. "I'm happy for you on that. I hope you can do it enough that Amber doesn't want to brain you any more than she did when you left."

He'd suggested that Amber get online and order herself some things to be delivered, like a coat, boots, and other warmer gear. When he'd told her to have them mailed to his house, she asked him what about her own home, and he told her to sell it. That was a big mistake. She'd only just got it from the courts, and here he was suggesting that she sell it off. Well, he'd told her to get rid of it, but that shouldn't matter. He was trying to make sense of their relationship still.

It was difficult for him to remember not to take his bad mood about people out on Amber. She would take it for only so long before she would blow up at him and yell at him. He was stunned when she did that. Not even his brothers had stood up to him when he'd been rude to them. And that was saying a great deal. He'd been pissing them off a lot longer than he had been Amber.

When he got back to his house, the aroma coming from the kitchen was something that he'd not smelled in a good long time. Steaks were being cooked in the kitchen, and he was suddenly starving to death. Going to see what was going on, Amber was setting the table in the big kitchen and telling him to wipe his feet.

It was on the tip of his tongue to tell her to back off; it was his home, but he caught himself just in time. As he was making sure that there wasn't any snow on his boots, he hung up his coat as well. There was no point in pissing her off even more.

Dinner was delicious and made more so because he hadn't had to cook. He never minded cleaning up, but cooking for him was a dirty chore, and he'd rather clean up dishes from a busy restaurant than have to cook for himself. Maybe, he thought, it would be nicer to cook for two with him and Amber than just himself. He'd have to give it a try sometime if she stayed with him.

They didn't know what they were doing. He knew that she'd be safer in his house. It was larger and had a solid front gate that no one could get through unless he wanted them to. Tomorrow, he was going to hire someone to be out there all the time, and that would keep away all the people he had only just realized. A win-win for him.

"I'll clean up." She told him that was good and she stood up to help him clean the table off. "I got this. You should go into the living room and have a nice seat while I do this. You cooked, which I hate doing by the way, and I'll clean up. I haven't hired a staff yet, as I was hoping to avoid it, but the house is just too much for one person to take care of and get anything done. And I have to work."

"I do as well." He explained to her that he really did need to work, to get the people in his mind to leave him alone. While she laughed at him, he smiled. No one had ever laughed at him in a long time, either. "I want to work. I know you have money, but that's yours. I have my own too. To make it last, I need to have a job. Besides, I don't think that I can just be a stay-at-home housewife either. It would drive me crazy."

"I don't want to start another fight with you, but my money is now all yours. What you have is yours too. But I will be putting your name on all that I own. Which is a bit more than my family knows about." She asked him if they knew that he wrote. "No. I suppose I should get around to telling them that, too. It's been hard on me to tell them much of anything, what with me being such a prick all the time."

"If you expect me to disagree with you about you being a prick, I'm not going to do it. You've been rude to me since we met. I know you're trying, but you have a long way to go." He nodded, trying his best not to let her words hurt him. And it did. Right in the heart. "Can I go with you when you talk to Lica? I wanted to talk to him about my mom and dad to see if he can help you, because it's doubtful that you'll ask for help in finding their killers."

"I'm not good at that, either." Guy also admitted that he didn't know how to approach the subject of him being an author either. "I've never told anyone. I know that Lica has a couple of my books on his shelf, and you have no idea how much I do want to know and don't want to know if he liked them or not."

"I can understand that. I don't know that I'd want to know either. But it's time you got some help with your emotions too, and what better people to let you know than those that love you." He asked her if she thought that they would tell him when he was being rude. Not that they didn't do that already. "I'm sure from what I know of them, they'll be a good deal nicer than you've been to them. We can only hope that you survive telling them what you think from now on. They might get it into their head to knock you around a bit."

"I think I would welcome that to having my head bashed in. There is no telling what I might see if someone were to do that again to me." She laughed, and he decided that it was a sound that he could get used to. Yes, he thought, he could get used to hearing her laughter all the time.

Chapter 4

"Did I borrow that from you?" Frustrated beyond anything he'd been before, Lica tried his best to keep up with what his brother was saying. "I didn't, did I? I mean, I remember buying that book at the bookstore when it came out."

"You're not listening to me. I wrote this book." For that, he got the book tossed into his face. "It's mine because I wrote it. Myself."

"But you're not Adam Sloan." He thought that he was making perfectly good sense and didn't understand why he wasn't getting it. "If you want to read it, I can lend it to you. But since I—" Brandy cut him off.

"I think what he's trying to tell you, darling, is that he is the author Adam Sloan and that he's been writing under that name for some time now." She looked at his brother. "Is that what you're trying to say? I must say, Guy, you have a wonderful character in this Dom Spark person. I read them myself and find that the writing is superb."

"Thank you, Brandy. It's been paying the bills

since I started." Lica wasn't going to let this go just because Brandy—

"I still don't understand. I know you always liked to write, but this man has put out some really good books. And I'm not saying that you couldn't do it, but there is no way that you've been writing under this name without any of us knowing it. Come on, Guy. Fess up. You're not Adam Sloan."

"What do I have to do—I have a check. It came to me today." He pulled out his mail, and Lica was creeped out by how far his brother would go to pretend that he was someone that he wasn't. There was no way that he kept it from them for all these… well, years. "Here. This is from two months ago. It's a nice one because I released a book then. My sales go up when I do that. But otherwise they're pretty good too."

The check was for just over twenty grand. He looked at his brother, trying his best to believe in him while being hurt that he'd never shared with them that he was a famous author. One that he himself read every time one of his books came out. Sitting in his chair again, he had to admit, he might well have been fooled. His brother was Adam Sloan.

Handing him back the check, he looked around the room. The others seemed to have gotten it before he did. But he thought that it was the secrecy of it all that had had him disbelieving his brother.

"I'm happy for you." Guy asked him what was wrong. "Nothing. I'm very proud of you. I would have been proud of you all along if you'd have told me. As it is now, I have to wonder what you were thinking every time I brought him up and told you about him that you were making fun of me."

"Never. I was in awe of you." Lica shook his head. "Yes, I was. You have no idea how hard it is for me to believe that anyone wants to read my books. It's like I'm putting out my heart and soul, and someone like you reads them. Not just once, but sometimes twice before the next book comes out. I've been humbled by your words of praise. Sometimes, I'm even embarrassed, too. And now I find out that you all were reading them. Well, I can't believe it. It's something that I never thought would happen."

"Why didn't you share that you were doing this?" He said that he had when they were broke, he would share the money from the check. "You told me you were working extra hours, that you had overtime money."

"I *was* working extra hours. And it *was* overtime money. I never stopped helping the family, Lica. I was there with everyone when things went good, too." He said he should have told them. "Why? You're not believing me now. How would you have reacted if I were to have told you that I was making good money as an author? Would you have had to have proof of it then, too? I'm telling you right now that I always gave more than what was fair to the family. I never shirked on my duty to you and the others."

"How do we know, since you more than likely kept that from us, too?" As soon as the words left his mouth, he regretted them. "I didn't mean that. Don't go, Guy. I'm sorry."

"This right here is why I didn't want you to know. This is why I don't like people. And in all the time saying that to you, I never once meant my family. Until today. Don't contact me for a while, Lica. I have a deadline to get to and I'd rather you not talk to me."

He couldn't get him to stay, no matter what he said to him. He didn't order him to say, though; it did occur to him that he could have, but that would have made things worse. Lica looked at Brandy for help.

"No, you did this on your own; you're going to have to fix it on your own as well. I can't believe you said that to him." He told her that he couldn't either. "Well, you'd better think of something before he decides to move away. And even as his brother, you'll never get him to return to the family. He might come here, Lica, but he won't feel as if he's part of this family again until you fix this."

"I was hurt." Brandy told him that he didn't hurt as badly as Guy looked like he did. "I know. I hurt him badly, and I have no one to blame but myself. I don't know what to do."

"Figure it out." Lica knew that he'd done a terrible thing. He wished that he could have believed in his brother right away like the others did. He just didn't want to believe that he'd kept something so personal about himself away from them all. And how he'd fucked up the relationship that they had together because he'd been...Lica couldn't believe it, but he'd been jealous of Guy and his success.

Trying to think how it had gone so wrong so quickly, he realized that he'd been the one who had caused it to go that way. Guy had tried to tell them something so important, and he'd just blown him off with his disbelief. He didn't want to believe that his brother could be so successful without his approval or something. That's what it was. He'd gone on to do something that he'd had no hand in, and he had been spiteful and mean to him. Grabbing his coat, he decided to go see his brother now before it was too late. He hoped that it wasn't, but he knew how badly he'd hurt his little brother.

On the way to the house, he tried to think of the way to say what he'd come to say. It wasn't going to be easy, he knew. And Guy wasn't going to make it easy on him. Not that he blamed him, but he'd been a prick, more so than Guy had been lately, and there wasn't anyone to blame but himself. As soon as Amber opened the door, he knew that Guy had told her what had happened as well.

"I've come to grovel at his feet." She told him to go away. "I should, but I can't. I have to fix this now before it's too late. I love him and don't know why— well, that's not true. I do know why I did that to him, but it doesn't make me feel any better about myself to know that I was jealous of my little brother. I should have figured it out when he was giving so much more money than could have been from overtime or working extra. I was a fool. Both then and now."

"He said that he didn't want to talk to you. Now I'd appreciate it if you were just to go back home and let him work." He asked if he was really working. "Of course he is. It's what he does when he wants to get some work done. What do you do? Order it to be done? Do you believe people when they tell you that they'll get it done on their own?"

"I deserve that. Can I please see him?" Lica would grovel to her as well if that was what it took. He'd hurt his brother, and he needed more than anything to make up to him. "I messed up, and I need to make it right. Please? Let me in so that I can see him to talk to him."

She finally stepped out from in front of the door. When he went inside, he was first shocked at the splendor of the home and then the hominess of the house. There were little touches of Guy and Amber throughout the room that he was standing in. As he went in search of his brother, hearing the clicking of keys through the house, he was once again struck with disbelief. This wasn't a house, it was a home. For two people whom he didn't think he knew all that well.

The colors were rich and warm. The furniture looked comfortable and cozy. The living room had soft lighting throughout. There were small touches on the end tables that looked perfect for the room. Lamps that weren't too bright for the warmth of the room. Blankets lay over the backs of the two couches and the three chairs. Pillows, something that he usually hated on a couch, looked good enough to take a nap on and feel rested on when you woke. The room was a perfect setting for family get-togethers and fun, as well as elegant at the same time.

The next room that he was in, Guy was there. With his head bent over the keyboard, it gave him the perfect opportunity to look around this room, too. The colors were bold. Hard reds and blues. Greens that looked like a meadow. The yellows blended into the room like they were a part of the walls and furniture. The desk looked like something that had been around for centuries; the lines and curves of it looked beautiful. When he realized that the typing had stopped, he looked at Guy.

"This is the most beautiful house I've ever been in. I love the colors and the way you've blended one room into the next effortlessly. It's like your stories. You do that equally well, and it's what keeps me reading them. Christ, Guy, you're very talented and I feel like a fool that I'm only just noticing just how wonderfully you've been weaving stories together even between us." He asked him what he wanted. "You. I want you back in my life. I want to know about your accomplishments and your perceived failures. Which, from my point of view, you never had. I can't believe I'm saying this, but I'd like to get to know the real you instead of the version you use to keep people at a distance."

"I don't like people." He said if they were half as bad as he'd been, then he didn't blame him. "I told you why I'm like that. To keep people from hurting me again. And you hurt me, Lica. All the way to the core of my heart."

"I know I did, buddy. And I will be sorry about that for the rest of my life. I should have taken your word for what you've been doing. I think you've been hinting at what you do all the time, and I never noticed. Or I didn't want to notice you. I'm profoundly sorry for the words that I said to you, and if you would forgive me, I'll never disbelieve you ever again." He was told that he had hurt him. "I did. I'll own that. I'm sorry, little brother. Please forgive me."

He bent over the computer again, and it felt like he was being dismissed. It was no less than he deserved. When he was ready to leave, Guy stopped him by saying his name. Lica braced himself for the words that were surely going to hurt him.

"I have copies of the next book that is coming out if you want them." He asked if it was book seventeen. "I don't know the number, but it's the next book. I have several copies that usually end up in my office because I don't have anyone to give them to."

"Sure, I'll take one. I'm betting that the others would like one as well." Guy explained that it wasn't out yet, so they couldn't share. "No, I wouldn't do that. You've given it to me; I'll treasure it forever."

"You didn't have to say that, Lica. I was going to give it to you anyway." He laughed and said that he really would treasure it if he signed it anyway. "I'll do that, but I'll sign it as Adam. That way, there's no misperception about who I am."

"Sure, sure, I understand. Which one are you working on now? Is it hard to get one started? How do you do it, with an outline? Where do you get such great idea—" Lica cut himself off this time. "I'm sorry. I have like a billion questions going through my mind right now. I can't seem to grasp any of them quickly enough to ask you."

For the first time in years, he'd bet maybe even longer, he heard his brother laugh. It was something that he'd not known he missed until right then. Going to the desk before he could change his mind, he pulled Guy from the seat he was sitting in and hugged him. He didn't let go until he hugged him back. Tears filled his eyes when he realized that was something else that he'd missed. Hugging his brother whenever he needed it.

"I'm sorry for a lot of things right now, Guy. I've missed so much. I don't know if it was your mood that I caused or just you pushing us away, but I'm not going to let that happen again. I've missed you and so much with you. I want to get to know you better again." He said that he'd like that too and told him that he was squeezing the life out of him. "I don't care. You should get used to it because this is going to be an everyday occurrence."

He finally let him go and stood staring at his brother before hugging him again. This time, Guy was quick to hug him back, and he was glad for it. He didn't want to squeeze the life out of him, but he would if necessary.

While he was closing down his computer, he answered his questions. Apparently, he'd been writing for years before he published his first Adam book.

As soon as he showed him the books that were still in boxes, he took one of each, trying to juggle them around so he'd not damage them. True to his word, Guy signed them all for him and even gave him one of the boxes to take them home in. Then they sat in the living room, his favorite part of the house so far, and talked to his brother about any topic that came to mind.

"I've never had such an enjoyable afternoon with anyone." Guy told him to stop sucking up. It was over now. "No, I wasn't sucking up, but I did want to tell you how much I've enjoyed this one-on-one time with you. It's been a real revelation for me."

"I won't lie to you, Lica." He said that he should have known that before today. "Yes, you should have. I might be successful at writing books, but I'm not good at people, and their hurting me. It's why I stayed away for so long. I don't like people, humans, or shifters, dead or alive. But now that I have a mate, I suppose I'll have to get over that soon."

"You have a mate?" He looked around the room and saw Amber walking down the hall. "Amber is your mate? That's great. How long have you known each other? Are you going to live here or…I'll shut up now."

"We've only known one another for about four days. She's staying here to get away from her brother and sister. They want the insurance policy that I was telling you about that she got the other day." He said that he remembered. "Look, why don't we order out some food, and you and Brandy, and the others come here for dinner. I've been wanting to show off my new home, and this will be the perfect time for me to get over some of my anxiety about being around people. Belinda said it would be good for me."

"Belinda is your mother-in-law?" He nodded. "I'm going to need your help on a few things. You have the ability to plot and stuff, so I was wondering what I should do about Bates." He told him everything that was going on with him and the bank with the elderly again. Just to reaffirm what he said to him the other day. That way, they were on the same page. "I'm losing money for the pack, and I don't want anyone to suffer anymore from him if I can help it. What should I do?"

"Kill him." He looked at his brother and asked him why. "He's disrespected you and your position. If you allow him to continue, he's going to undermine you in a lot of things. Kill him and anyone that he's working with."

"I thought you were joking before when you told me that." Guy just shook his head and pointed out that Bates needed to die to make an example of people that fucked with him to show that he's not a pushover.

"Do you think that I am?"

"It's not me that you have to impress this upon. I know you're all badass and all, but the people being taken advantage of are thinking that you're just a big blowhard that doesn't care about the people he's responsible for." He asked him again if he thought that. "Again, I'm not the one you have to impress with yourself. You and Brandy both need to confront him, kill him and his family, and be done with it. If there are others, which I'm sure there are, then you deal with them the same way. I would just walk up to him and his family and rip their throats out. At least that's what I'd do if someone was messing around in my pack."

They talked about the things that Bates was doing, and it occurred to him that Guy was right. There was too much that he had his hand in that was disrupting his ability to run a good pack. Or at least one that cares about his people. First thing tomorrow, he was going to find him and kill him. Just like he said to do it too. Just rip his throat out and be done with him.

When the rest of the family arrived, Brandy and the other women were making plans about dinner. They all, like him, marveled at the house and the fact that he'd only lived in it for about three months. It was the most put-together home he'd ever been in, and Lica never wanted to leave. He talked to his brothers about

Bates, and they agreed with Guy. Kill him so that he was no longer an issue.

"I'm with you, but let's please go as a family unit. I'm willing to do my part in this as well, but I want to have backup just in case." He told Brandy that he had planned on it. "Good. Now, while we're talking, you need to have a second. I don't think there is anyone better for the job than Guy. He's on point in giving you information that you need, and he's right in this thing with Bates. I'll work with Amber to see if she could be my second as well."

"Deal." He pulled Brandy into his arms and held her tightly before speaking again. "She might tell you no, but I've dealt with her today; you talk her into doing it for the two of us."

"All right." The rest of the night went well. Guy gave them a plan to follow in getting things finished up with the elderly. He needed to assign someone who would be there for them after this was done. Someone whom he trusted with money. It wasn't anything for him to assign his brother Edmond and Mac the job. They'd do a good job with them and be as honest as much as Bates was a thief.

~*~

Guy stood next to his brother as they knocked on the door to the Bates home. It was much nicer than he thought it should have been for a man who said retiring was going to cost him more than he had. The house looked like it had several wings off the back, no doubt where his two sons and their families were living.

Belinda had found out that the wives were about as clueless about the way things were being run as a newborn would have knowledge of where his bottle was coming from. Wilma Bates, however, was right there with her husband in making sure that things were run just like they'd been when her husband had been Alpha.

Playing at being retired had offered Lincoln the opportunity to be more behind the scenes. He could spend his money the way that he wanted, and no one was the wiser. Living in the big house on a lot of property, too, gave him the illusion of being out of things that he was stealing from the pack.

But they had a list, and according to pack law, he had to be read what he was doing wrong before anyone could kill him. Guy would have said fuck the bylaws, but he wasn't one to follow rules when it came to making things work out the way that he wanted. He was going to have the pleasure of reading him the things that they had on the list, which included about twenty-five things that were involved in other things around the pack. Like the missing food from the pantry. Money from the bank, as well as having his hand in the school projects that had been deemed wrong by the pack, without them knowing it.

"Lica? What do we owe this unplanned visit to? My wife and I were just headed out to the Amish country." He started reading the list that they had after demanding that the entire household come to the living room. "You're making me very nervous. And with my bad heart, that's not a good thing to be doing."

Guy continued reading the list of things and telling what his part in the plots was. After about four of them being read, Bates asked what the meaning of this was. Guy was happy to tell him, but it was Lica who needed to say that part. They were following the book in this crap so that nothing came back to bite them in the butts.

"You've been given a list, Lincoln, and the penalty for each. Now I will sentence you. Death by alpha. Because I *am* the alpha." Whatever Bates was going to say was cut off by the swipe of the hand of the most powerful man he knew. Bates' wife suffered the same death, and so did their two sons and wives. At the last minute, Belinda found that the women had been shopping with the ill-gotten gains just the day before.

After the cleanup, it was just a simple thing to have their bodies on display outside their home. Lica met with the crowd that had gathered. Word had spread fast that Bates and his entire family had been killed, and the list of crimes was there for all to read. It was a grisly way to end a life, but it had the effects that were needed to get the pack behind him once again.

"Starting today, anyone who was working with Bates and his entire family will be treated to the same death unless you come to me and tell me why you thought it was a good idea to rob from the very pack that supplies you with sustainable life gifts." That was his part in his speech, and it seemed to go over as well as he thought it should. Lica told him that if there were any more deaths from this, it would be on him and Amber to do them. He was fine with that, as was Amber when she heard what had been going on behind their backs in the pack. She might well have killed the other had she been allowed to do it. She was fired up.

After telling the people what was going to happen from now on, there was a general nervousness that was expected. People didn't look around at their fellow pack members, and he thought that was very telling. They weren't going to be giving away if they knew someone else was going to have to die today.

The meeting and the questions afterwards took up most of the morning. The elderly were happy to find out that they could get their checks cashed without having to pay for it. They were also excited to know that they weren't going to be charged double the prices at the grocery store. Brandy was going to be bringing in another store that would start right away with things that were needed. They were running it from the pantry.

Since the grocery store owner wasn't pack, then he'd have to be dealt with by someone else. It was Summer who made a few calls to the Feds to get him taken care of for not claiming the real money he made off the pack members. They were also able to find the book of names for the pack that he would use to charge more to them.

"The post office has been notified, and as soon as checks start to come in, they'll notify my office, and I'll make sure that they're cashed and brought to you. If you need anything from town, call my office. If you simply need someone to talk to after all this, call my office. I'm going to be more hands-on than I've been so far, so expect to see a great deal more of my wife and me, plus my family. We're going to take a deep interest in what is going on around here. So if you're screwing up or making trouble, you can bet that I'm going to be finding out. I have eyes everywhere."

One man in the back stood up from the hastily brought in chairs. He looked around the room, then right at Lica. He was proud of his brother for not shifting around on his feet, but he could tell that he was nervous. He was, too. Mr. March had a way about him that made you think that he was a man who got answers.

"I have me a list of things that need to be done at my house. I'm about the oldest man in this pack and would like for you to assign some younger pups to help me around the place." Lica told him that it was in the works, and he had a signup sheet for those who needed help. "Will we be paying out the ass for this help? I don't have me nothing but my pension, and it don't go as far as I'd like for it to."

"The help for the elderly will be given to them so long as they're in good standing. And right now, there is a clean slate for those who need help." Mr. March started to sit down, but stopped himself with a look to his brother again. He told him that he could use someone around to help him sort his pills and such. "Whatever you need, Mr. March. We'll be there for you and the rest of the pack. So long, as I said, you were in good standing."

"Mr. March, I'll be over first thing in the morning to help you with your pills. Do you need them picked up for you, or do you have that?" Summer looked at Lica and smiled. "With two little girls, I have to be good at organizing things. I'll gladly help out whoever needs it when it comes to helping with medications."

There were a few show of hands of people who needed that sort of help. The signup sheet was sent around, and people were happy to put their names on the list to work. There was a lot of interest in things that needed to be taken care of, too. Then Mr. March stood up again.

"I mean you no disrespect, young man, but I'm glad to see you got your head out of your ass and did this to Bates. He was nearly killing off the elderly in this pack by thinking that we don't have anything to offer and we're too stupid to have an opinion about shit going on. But we've been around a while and know things that would boggle the young people's minds if we were allowed to have a say once in a while." Lica asked him if he wanted to head up the elderly help sheet to get things done. "I can do that. I don't suppose there will be any pay for this help I'm giving?"

"Everyone will be paid who works for the pack." Again, he said so long as they were in good standing. It was something that he suggested that he'd have people sign up for things, thinking that they'd be able to pull the wool over their eyes. With Belinda's help, they were getting a few people taken care of who, while not as bad as Bates but they needed to be arrested for the crimes they'd been committing.

Chapter 5

"Where have you been?" Shawn just stared at Margaret until she looked at him. "I've not seen you all morning. Where have you been?"

"I've been at the hospital since yesterday. I was there trying to get something to stop the bleeding of these wounds—do you mean to tell me you didn't miss me at all last night? I'm your brother."

"I know who you are, Shawn. It's just that when I went to bed, you weren't here, and when I woke up, you were gone again. How was I supposed to know that they meant the same outing? Did you have fun at least?" There were days like today when he would gladly have strangled his sister to death. "I've been busy too. Did you know that when you write a check at the bank, they'll give you cash for it?"

"I did know that, yes. Did you happen to have a good reason to go to the bank, Margaret? There was just enough money in the account for us to have dinner tonight." She said that they let her close out the account for the two hundred dollars that was in the account. "And the reason you closed out the account? You do know that we need every penny we can save until we can get the money from Amber, right? I did tell you that, didn't I?"

"You did, but the checks were just there. I know you said something about needing to have money in the account for the checks to work, but I don't understand that. You have hundreds of checks, Shawn. If they closed out the account, we can still write those checks on the account. That's why they gave us the checks in the first place, so we can use them to write for money." He told her again that it didn't work that way. "So says you."

"So says everyone who has ever opened an account. With you closing the account out, that means that the checks aren't any good anymore. Now we are well and truly fucked over because of you." She waved him off like whatever he said didn't matter. "It does matter, Margaret. What are we going to do about food for the next few nights?"

"We'll write checks. Don't be silly, Shawn. You know that I'm right. You have something wrong with you in regard to the checks, don't you? I can write them from now on if you don't want to. It's quite easy. Even the lady at the bank said I do a good job with them. She told me that not many people use the memo part of the checks, but it helps you understand why you wrote out the check in the first place. See? I know all about them."

Except for the fact that they were useless if you didn't have any money in the account, he thought. "You can order tonight, and I'll write the check. That way you can get what you want and we'll both be happy."

He just walked away from her. It was that or he was really going to strangle her for being such an idiot sometimes. Sitting in his chair, he put his hand over the marks on his chest that the big dog had given him. They wouldn't stop bleeding, no matter how many different kinds of stitches or tapes they put over them. Not until he told the dog that he was sorry. But he had to mean it when he said it. Stupidest thing that he'd ever heard. Where you could be marked by something and not let it heal until you apologize for it. He'd never apologized for anything in his life; he wasn't going to do that with a fucking dog.

Dozing in his chair, he was woken up once by the front doorbell going off. Knowing how much his sister loved going to the door, he didn't even bother getting awake enough to see who it was. A while later, there was another person at the door, and it took him three rings before he realized that no one was going to get it.

Getting up, he made his way to the door to see who would be disturbing his naptime. As soon as he saw the police there, he knew something had happened to his sister. She never left the house without him, and since she had not answered the door, she must be in trouble.

"What's happened to her?" The officer looked shocked that he asked that, and told him he was here about something else. "My sister isn't here. She's the one who would be responsible for whatever you have a problem with. I've been here all morning."

"We're here about the reported stolen car. We know that it was repossessed last month. You would know that too, so why did someone report it stolen?" He asked who had claimed that it had been. "Margaret Gross. She said that she went out to get her car, and it was missing. Presuming that it was stolen, she called us."

"She gets things mixed up once in a while. I'll have a talk with her." The officer said that it was a false report. "I promise you that it won't happen again. Like I said, she gets confused sometimes. I'll talk to her, and you won't hear about the car again. She's not here right now, but I will as soon as she comes home."

"See that you do." He wanted to tell the man that he said he would and slam the door in his face, but didn't. Shawn didn't need any more trouble right now. "Did you know that you're bleeding?"

"Yes, I did know that. I just spent too many hours to count at the emergency department to get it fixed, and they couldn't do anything for it." He asked if he'd been cut by a shifter. "Yes, a dog."

"Wolf. You smell like one of the Frazier men. Could be you bit off more than you could chew, I'm thinking. Nice men, you must have pissed one of them off powerfully for them to let you bleed like that." The nurse at the emergency department said the same thing to him last night. Like he cared how much they were pissed off. "I'd be thinking of a way to tell them how sorry you are for whatever you did before you bleed to death." He tipped his hat and told him to have a good day before leaving with the man he came with.

As gently as he could, he shut the door and waited until he counted to twenty three times before he let go of the scream that he'd been holding for what seemed like his whole life. Then he went in search of his sister.

She wasn't hard to find. She was in her room writing out checks for the bills that were overdue, or they'd already gotten turned off. He, just as calmly as he could, asked her what she was doing.

"I'm getting our things back. I already called the dealership and told them that I paid off one of the cars. You'll have to give me your stuff so that I can pay off yours. I mailed out a lot of checks today, Shawn. You should have put me in charge of our bills from the beginning. I'm doing such a good job at keeping things running." She was currently stuffing an envelope that went to the electric company, and he just let her. "I'm using a lot of the checks that we had. I hope that I don't run out before I get everything paid."

"I don't either. Because you know that once the checks are gone, there isn't any more money." She just grinned at him, telling him that he'd just have to order more. She even handed him the form that came with the checks to order them through the bank. "Yes, I'm sure they'll be thrilled to charge us for more checks on an account that's closed."

He left her to it. There wasn't any way that anything was going to be paid off with the way things were going. Not only that, but even if they got the money from Amber, they didn't have an account to put the money in as of right now. At least they'd eat well tonight with the cash she'd gotten from the account. Nothing else to do but go with her way of doing things. For now, at least.

It took him nearly three hours to get things in order in the kitchen. Margaret acted as if they still had staff and a great deal of them by the way the kitchen looked when he'd gone into it. She even left the lid off the milk container when she'd been 'cooking' herself some cereal. That was the extent of her cooking: pouring some cereal into a bowl and serving herself. After the kitchen, he went back to the living room.

Sitting in his chair again, he thought about what

he was doing. There wasn't any way he was going to be able to show his face at any of the clubs that they used to go to all the time. And as of last month, he couldn't get himself there unless he walked. And he hated the snow and cold. He didn't much care for the heat and rain either, but one season at a time was all he could work with right now.

All his nice clothing was at the dry cleaners, and he couldn't get them out without cash. The check thing hadn't worked out so well for him last month when he'd tried to pay with a check like his sister was doing right now.

He really needed to talk to Amber and see if she'd give them some of the insurance money that she'd gotten from their mom. Why she did that to them was something that he wished he could ask her. She'd literally left them out in the cold with the way things were going in their life. But Amber was their only solution to getting back on track.

Picking up the phone, he tried to calm his heart down from being so afraid to call her. He'd never been afraid of anything concerning Amber, and right now, he was worried that her soon-to-be husband would come around and finish the job he'd started the other night. Killing him off didn't sound like such a bad option right now. Now, with his sister committing mail fraud as well as the hundreds of dollars in bounced check charges they were going to incur while she was making things 'right' for them. He just didn't know what to do.

As soon as the phone was answered, he didn't think it was the Frazier person he asked to speak to Amber. Everything that he had planned out to say to her went out the door the moment she said 'hello' to him. Sobbing out what was going on in his life, how Margaret was going to ruin them, he found himself on the floor in the living room, curled up into the fetal position, sobbing about how he didn't know if he was going to make it and needed her help.

"How much do you need? I'm not saying that I'll help you, you've been a right bastard to me all my life, but you tell me how much you need and I'll think about helping you. And for the love of god, take the checkbook away from Margaret before she digs you a hole you'll never see the light of day again through." He told her that he didn't know how much he needed, and that was the truth. He figured that asking for money and getting it was far between, but she wasn't hanging up on him, so he gave her a good estimate. "That's a great deal of money, Shawn. How did you get so far behind?"

"I'd like to blame it all on Margaret, but that wouldn't be true. She's not helping our situation, but then neither had I been." He told her how their electricity and cable were going to be cut off, and thankfully, the house phone was working now, or he'd have not been able to call her to beg. And begging he was. "I don't care about the cars getting back to us, nor about the cable. I can't remember the last time I sat down to watch a movie. We need just enough to cover the basics. Phone, electricity, and some money for food. Though I'm not sure who would cook it. The staff left us about six weeks ago, and we've been living off of cereal and microwave food. That crap is nasty. So I guess we've been eating out when we should have been cooking at home. Just help me keep the power on and get our phones back to working. I can deal with not having the rest."

"I'll do that, but it'll come with a cost." He didn't care if she wanted his left foot right now; he'd do anything to have one thing go right. "You have to be nice to me. I don't mean until the power is kept on, but all the time. I've never done anything to you, and I don't like the way you treat me when you feel as if I owe you something."

"All right. I can do that. But you have to work with me on that. I'm not going to be able to change overnight. Please?" She told him so long as he was trying, she'd work with him. "You have no idea how much I appreciate this, Amber. I know that we've been a shit to you before, but I'm going to change. I don't

know about Margaret. She's...I think that there is
something wrong with her mind. She doesn't seem to
understand about banks and checks."

He told her what she was doing again and
again, and he was told to stop her. But he figured that
if anyone were to spend ten minutes with her, they'd
see that there was something very wrong with his twin
sister.

After hanging up with Amber, with the promise
to meet him at the power office in an hour, she was
going to pick him up and take him there. It was more
than he could have hoped for, and he told her that. As
soon as he got off the phone, he went to find Margaret
again. Apparently, writing checks wasn't something
that she liked anymore, and she was arranging the
furniture in her room.

"I have to make room for my stuff." He asked
her what stuff. "You know, stuff that I had before. The
ones that we had to sell for money."

"We still don't have any money, Margaret." She
said that she counted and they have fifty-three checks
left. "Yes, would you mind if I took over those for
now? And I'll see that these get put in the proper place
for mailing."

"Don't forget to get stamps. I have a check
already saved out for that. The one with your favorite
movie on it." He'd forgotten about them ordering

checks that were movie-themed. He did wonder now why they'd done that. Just to spend money, he figured. "Are you going out?"

"I am. I have to see someone about the power before they shut it off." He hoped they'd get there before it was turned off. They wanted to charge him an extra two hundred and fifty dollars to have it turned back on again. "You stay here, and I'll be back soon, and we can order out. As a celebration."

"Yes, because I've gotten us out of debt now. Silly brother. I told you to do this at the beginning." Yes, he thought there was something wrong with his sister. "Now we'll get our things back and go on like we did before. I can't stand being broke all the time, Shawn. It's not good for me."

"What do you mean?" She told him that she couldn't sleep at night the way that he was doing things, that she had to be in charge of something like the bills, so that they'd not be stressed out. "I was stressed out. I'm glad that you've taken some of the burden off my shoulders."

He had to get out of her room. It hurt his heart when he thought of how much stress she'd been under, and his stress levels were higher because he had to take care of her. Going to the front door to wait on Amber, he thought of all the things that he'd had planned and were now useless because he'd been...they'd been so useless with money. What the hell was wrong with them?

It wasn't as if they had grown up with a great deal of money. They had a comfortable life. Had anything that they wanted, whether they needed it or not. But after killing their dad, then their mom, they'd gotten stupider. It occurred to him that he might get into trouble for killing them, but he didn't dwell on it for long. He had enough on his mind right now without thinking of going to prison for killing his parents.

True to her word, Amber came by to pick him up and take him to the electric power company. He wasn't thrilled that she'd brought Frazier with her, but she was doing him a favor, and he wasn't going to complain. While he sat in the back seat, she told him what was going to happen with the power company.

"I called, and we have to pay off the entire bill before they don't shut it off. That's a bit more than you told me." He told her how he'd only just gotten a past due notice yesterday, and that was the amount on it. "They're making you pay the current bill, too. The cell service was a good deal nicer about it. I had to pay the remaining amount owed on the phones that you both got, and then this month's bill. A bit more there, too, but they were kind enough not to say it would cost you an arm and a leg to keep your service on. So that's paid."

"Thank you." He could actually feel some of the stress rolling off his back. "I've put the checks away that Margaret wrote. She just wrote them out for every bill that we had. Some of them were for magazine subscriptions that I didn't know we got, but she said that she'd done it, so I'm going to assume that they'll have to wait a bit longer or just stop sending them to us."

After going to the power company and paying that bill, they headed to the cell service and had that bill changed around so that they were no longer paying on the phones they'd gotten. Only the best was what they'd gotten for themselves, and he couldn't remember a single thing that his phone did that he thought he needed at the time. He couldn't even remember the last picture that he took with it, and it was supposed to have a state-of-the-art camera with it.

He was surprised when Amber and her husband, whose name he still didn't know, took him out to lunch. He thought about Margaret but decided that, for today, she could eat cereal. It was all the two of them had been eating for several days now, as the microwave stuff hadn't been as easy as it said it would be on the package. He was giddy to be out to lunch, too, with someone other than his twin.

"I'm going to give you some money to keep you afloat, but you're going to have to get yourself a job." He nearly snarled at her that he wasn't going to be low enough to get that when he realized that she was helping now. If he didn't help himself, then she'd not help him now. "Also, the cars that have been repossessed are going to have to be paid off, too. Along with other things that you've gotten when you didn't have any income."

He was handed a pen and a small notebook to write things down in. However, about the second page of notes, he had to stop and shove it all away. Amber and Fraizer looked at him sharply.

"I need to back off for a moment. I'm not used to...I'm trying my best to be nice here, but it's too much." She said she understood. "I don't understand any of this. I was just thinking before you came to get me that I don't know where it came from in my mind that I had to have such expensive things. And that I needed the best of the best, no matter the cost. I'd like to blame it all on you, but that's not going to work. You never had anything to do with us spending money like we had it. I want to blame it all on you. I won't, but that's where my head is going right now."

He wanted to cry and had to work hard on not doing that. Shawn knew that he was a grown man and had to take responsibility for things that he'd created. It wasn't anyone's fault that he was where he was but himself. He looked at Fraizer when he said his name.

"I don't know what to do about any of this. Asking for help was something that I never thought would happen. I thought that I had it under control. That when the money was gone, then I'd just get more. Where, you might ask? I have no idea, but I thought that it would just be there, like it had been when I was a kid, and that would supply us with whatever we needed. I need to grow up." Frazier said his name again. "I'm sorry. So very sorry for anything and everything that I did to you to piss you off enough that you cut me. I know that it's not enough, just saying that I'm sorry, but I'm in so deep right now that I don't even know if when I wake tomorrow that this isn't going to start all over."

"I forgive you." Something akin to the room tightening like it did the night he'd been attacked happened again. This time, he ran his hands over his chest to feel that the wounds were finally closed. Thankfully, too, he was bleeding through his shirts faster than he could keep them clean. "There's a job opening at the local slaughterhouse that you can have. It pays well, but it's a shit job."

"I'll take it." He'd never worked a job in his life, but he knew that he had to do something. Then he thought of Margaret being on her own while he worked. "I have to do something with Margaret. I don't think she's mentally right in the head. I don't know that she's mentally challenged, but there is something wrong about her thinking."

"I have a couple of connections. I'll call one of them and see if they can have a look at her for you." He thanked Fraizer. "My name is Guy. You can call me Fraizer if you want, but that's my first name."

"I'm sorry again." He was told not to worry about it, that it was fine. "No, it's not. If I'm screwing up, I want to know. I can't begin to fix myself if I don't work on the little things at the beginning of this journey."

They talked a bit more until it was apparent that they were going to be at the restaurant when the next shift showed up. He didn't mind. Someone was waiting on him, and it had been a long time since he'd had such a luxury. It would be a long time coming again, the way things were going, but he wasn't going to dwell on the things that he didn't have, only the ones that he had now. And right now, he had a lot of things that he never thought he'd have again. Friendship was one of those things that he'd never had. He didn't count Margaret because she was related to him, but he did like the fact that Amber was being so nice to him, as well as Guy.

When someone else showed up to take him to the slaughterhouse, he was willing to go with them, but nervous too. He didn't have a lot of male friends—

hell, he didn't have any friends — but he knew that he was going to have to do this if he ever wanted to get ahead again. Going with Edmond to the house, he was both relieved and terrified of what the next step in his journey was going to be.

"You've never worked before, have you? The reason I asked is because you took the first job offered to you, and you could have questioned this one." He told him that his brother said that it paid well. "It does at that. But it's a shitty job. I'll be the first to admit that. We all work there but Ayden. He has other ventures that he does for Brandy and the family."

"Like I said, I'll do whatever it takes to get me back to some sort of living wage where I can pay my own way." Edmond nodded. "I've really fucked up my life. I guess you know that. You and your family can talk to one another through that mind thing you have."

"You mean Guy? No, he didn't tell me anything other than you needed a job and were willing to work with us." He glanced at him. "You don't mind working with us, do you? We're all right, men with a good head on our shoulders."

"I've heard that about you." He'd heard a great deal about the Fraizer men, but he'd never taken the time to really listen to what was being said. He said as much to the man with him. "I was sort of on this self-destruction way of living, and it finally caught up with me. My life has been all fun and games until it wasn't. When we received the money from when my father died, we, meaning my sister and I, went a little overboard. We didn't ever once think of tomorrow, but only the right then. I suppose people don't act like we did when they get a bit of money."

"You'd be surprised. I think that humans are crazy with all kinds of things that they probably think that I am as well. As a shifter, we've had to lay low for all of our lives, yet be out there to make a living as well. It's never going to be easy as a shifter, but we're making it work for us." He told him that it shows. "Thanks. We owe a great deal to our way of living now to Brandy, Lica, my older brother's wife, for how we're doing now. She made sure that we knew there was money to be had and how to make more. It's been a real eye-opener since she came into the family."

"I'd like to say that no one taught us how to live with money, but that would be a lie. We didn't listen was what our problem was. And if we did listen, it was to hear things that we wanted to hear that had nothing to do with reality." He thought of some of the things that he'd been known to spout off, like all kinds of things that were going on with the government. He decided that he was going to start watching the news more and reading more than just the vanity page in the paper. That had been getting him nowhere.

"I just heard from Guy. He wanted me to tell you that you can take your sister to the clinic tomorrow, and his friend and doctor will be there to evaluate Margaret." He thanked the other man. "Also, he said to tell you that there will be someone to pick you up daily when you have to go to work. There will be a car in your driveway to keep you from having to walk in the snow starting next week. He just has to get one lined up for you to use."

"Thanks." He had to turn away, his eyes filling with tears again. They were being so good to him, he hoped that once things started falling into place, he'd not turn back to the way he'd been before. Although he didn't really know this for sure, he thought that if he didn't do what was necessary to make things right, he'd not live long. Guy or any one of his brothers would take him out as surely as he was sitting in this nice car. Of that, he had no doubt.

After being shown around the place, he was taken home. There was a car in the driveway, nothing that he'd ever have bought for himself, but it looked like it would be good in the snow and get him around where he needed to be. There was also a note with it. Telling him that he wasn't to allow Margaret to drive it until the tests were run on her. He knew that wouldn't be all that hard; she never drove anywhere anyway.

Chapter 6

Amber wasn't sure how to handle this new Guy. He was acting like a wounded dog, no pun intended, she thought to herself. He was apologetic and quiet. While he would answer her if she had any questions, he didn't seem to have much in the way of opinions either. She flat-out didn't care for this man that he'd become.

"I have to go write for a while." That was another thing. When he said that he had to write for a while, he meant just that. If he didn't go and sit at his computer for a few hours at a time working like a man possessed, he'd be antsy and sulky—more than before. Always looking at the door to his office in a forlorn sort of way. Again, she didn't care for this man. She thought that she'd like the rude man just so she didn't feel bad when she took him to task. "I'll be in my office if you need me."

"I do need you." Guy didn't move but glanced at the door again, like it were almost an escape from talking to her. "I need you to have sex with me. I need it like it's my next breath."

"Sex?" She nodded at him, and when he smiled,

she could tell it was forced. "Would you like to have it now? I mean, I'm always willing if that's what you want."

"What do you want?" He seemed to be confused by the question. "Do you want to have sex with me? Or are you happy with the arrangements that we have going on right now?"

"I never thought about it." He looked sheepish for a second before he looked at her again. "I mean, I've thought about it. A great deal, but I don't want you to feel like I'm forcing you." He looked away towards the door again. "I think that's the reason that I write so much while you're here. So I don't jump you when you get close to me."

"Why didn't you ever say anything to me before?" He shrugged. "Guy? Tell me why you didn't say anything before? Is it me?"

"No, it's not you, but me. I'm...I'm—fuck. I'm trying so hard to be what you want me to be that I feel as if I'm losing a part of myself to trying to be this other person that you need me to be. I can be that way, but I find that I'm thinking too hard on what I want to say and discarding everything in favor of not blowing up." He grabbed the door jam, and she could see his fingers digging deeply into the wood. "I don't want to be rude, but there are times when I feel as if I can't talk to you because I'm afraid of saying the wrong thing.

Like, there are things that I want to talk to you about that I can't because of the hold you have over me."

"I never wanted you to be a different person. I just wanted to be able to have a conversation with you and you not biting my head off." He told her that he didn't have any idea how to do that anymore. "So you want to be rude all the time."

"No. Damn it, that's not what I said at all." He started down the hall, and she thought that he was leaving her, but all he did was pace it. She watched as he mumbled to himself something about rudeness getting him nowhere. "I'm learning here. Or trying to learn how to be this person that everyone wants me to be. But I'm not a person anymore. I don't know that I ever was. I never thought of myself as being rude, but just blunt. Sort of in the mindset that if you ask me a question, I'm going to give you the answer, whether it hurts your feelings or not. I'm beginning to see that I could have tempered it a bit, but I'm lost in the process of being this entirely different man than I want to be."

"So you thought that not talking at all was the way to go." He stared at her, and she could see that it was exactly what he thought. "I want you to be able to talk to me. I would love to talk to you about your day, but getting one syllable words out of you doesn't feel right either."

"You want to know how my day is going? It's

shit if you want to know the truth. I have this beautiful mate in my home, and I'm wondering all the time if she'd rather be in her own home. So you know, if that's what you want, I'll live wherever you want to go. But I can't ask you because I'm forever thinking how to say something to you until the moment is gone." He washed his hand over his face as he continued. "I'm sleeping down the hall from you, and all I can think about is that we should be sharing a bed. Not even counting on sex to play into it, just sleeping together would be wonderful. I have this book that plays on my mind a great deal, too, but it keeps getting messed up with having you beneath me. I want to solve Belinda's murder, too, but I don't know how to get started on it without stepping on a lot of toes and pissing people off. Did you know that the police have a video of the murder, but they don't know how to figure out who it is? Not to mention, your brother and sister did it. How will that go over with you, knowing that the man we just got out of some of his debt is a murderer twice over? He has it in his head that he killed your father, too. Just because he had mentioned once that he had some insurance on himself that would take care of them after he was gone. What sort of sick kid does that when they're only about thirteen years old? I don't know the answer to that either. I have all this shit in my head, and the only one that I can think of most of the time is making love to you."

"I'd very much like that too." She thought about what he'd told her about Shawn. "I don't know what to do about my brother either. Nor Margaret. Did I tell you that the doctor said that she has the mentality of someone about half her age? That's about the time she killed mom." She started toward him. "How about we take care of these issues by importance. You and I will make love, and then we'll tackle the other things. One at a time."

She stood in front of him as he held onto the wall. If he kept up with digging his nails into the wood, they were going to need more than just a makeover, but new walls put in. Reaching up, she pulled his hand off the wall and put it around her waist. Leaning in, she kissed him on the mouth gently before moving to his throat. His low growl made her wet just like that.

"What do you suppose sex with me is going to resolve? I'm betting not much. I've not had a lot of practice at making love. For some reason, women were turned off by my ordering them around."

"You can order me around all you want." Running her hand down his chest to his cock, she cupped him in her hand. "Like you could order me to suck your cock for you until you come all over me and I'd do it to the best of my abilities."

Guy rolled his hips so that her hand filled with

his cock. As he gently fucked her hand, she used her free one to undo the buttons on the front of his shirt. Once she had that finished, he didn't move until she was pulling it free of his pants and running her hand over his muscles there.

"You're all right with me ordering you around in the bedroom." She said she was all right with him ordering her around, no matter where they were having sex. "You want me right here in this hallway? Do you really want me to come all over you?"

"Oh yes, I do very much so." Getting down on her knees to prove what she wanted from him, she was working his belt open when he put his hand on her head. "Tell me what you want, Guy. I'm here to please you."

"Take my cock into your mouth and suck me." His voice was rough and hard. It made her pussy gush with wetness that she knew he could smell when his nostrils flared. "Before you take my cock into your mouth, I want you to strip down to your warm body so that I can see what I'm getting."

She was so wet when she pulled her panties off first. Tossing them through the air, he caught them up in his hand and took them to his face. Christ, that movement alone had her coming with a short, hard punch to her system that had her leaning against his body until she could see straight again.

"Next time you come without me telling you, you'll be punished. Do you understand me?" She said that she did, but she no longer recognized her own voice when she spoke. "Strip down to nothing right now."

Hurrying through the process of taking off her clothing made her clumsy. Once she had her blouse off, she sat there stupidly, not having any idea where to go next. His small growl had her taking off her bra and skirt so that she was just as naked as he wanted her to be. Without a word to him, she undid his pants and freed his cock.

He was so thick that she couldn't put her fingers around him and have them touch. Licking his crown, she stuck her tongue into the tiny eye and played with him. Cupping his balls into her hand, she marveled at their warmth and fullness as she took his cock into her mouth.

His knees shook against her body. She wasn't sure if he was having a difficult time standing up or what was going on with him. As she swallowed him down past the tightness of her throat. She knew a feeling that she'd never felt before. It was the best feeling in the world. Guy put his hand on the back of her head and held her there while he fucked her mouth and throat.

"Touch your pussy." Gladly, she thought and

moved her hand down to her own femininity. The heat coming off herself was amazing. As she slid her fingers into her sheath, she moaned and then heard Guy growl. Whatever she'd done, she was going to do it again to have him fucking her this way. Humming a tune that she didn't know the words to, she knew he was having a hard time keeping pace as he pulled free of her mouth.

The first bit of cum splashed her in the face. The next was her lips and mouth. Even as he fisted his cock, she helped by fondling his balls and hoping to have them empty completely on her. Rubbing the cum into her breasts, she nearly missed him telling her to stop when he did. Christ, she was on fire for him to allow her to come.

"Stand up." She did so, but apparently not fast enough. He grabbed her by the hair and pulled her right up off the floor. Before she could remember not to come, she was crying out with the release that had her nearly buckling to the floor again. Then she felt the wood of the wall behind her when he pressed her into it. "I'm going to fuck you."

"Yes." He lifted her up just enough that she could feel her pussy at his groin. When he slammed deep inside of her, she cried out again, but more for pain than pleasure. As soon as he started plowing her — there was no other word for it, she put her hands over his shoulders and held on. Bumping her head on the wall, she bit her lip, trying to keep herself from coming again without his permission.

Nuzzling her throat, she laid back her head, giving him whatever he wanted. As soon as his tongue slid over her pounding pulse, she knew that he was going to bite her. Leaning more to give him all of her, she screamed when his teeth grazed over her throat. Closing her eyes to the onslaught of emotions and colors swirling around her head, she lost consciousness when he bit down on her neck just below her ear.

It couldn't have been more than a few seconds that she'd fainted, but when she woke up, Guy was coming deep inside of her. Digging her nails into his shoulders, she held onto him as he licked at her throat once again and told her he had her. The next thing she knew, he was coming a second time and telling her — no commanding her to come with him.

Amber had had sex before. She'd even had a couple of climaxes, but nothing could have prepared her for the assault of emotions that caught her breath. It didn't just catch her breath, but took it away and stopped her heart from beating at the same time. Then once again she lost consciousness.

When she woke, she was in the biggest bed she'd ever seen. And lying right next to her was Guy. He was leaning on his hand, staring at her. She'd never been so embarrassed in her life until that moment. Leaning in, he kissed her on the mouth before smiling at her.

"I've never done anything like that before. Being rough during sex. Did I hurt you?" She said she was kind of afraid to move right now. "I'm sore, all over my body. I think, too, I might have pulled some of your hair out. I'm profoundly sorry for that, too."

"Let me get up and go to the bathroom." He didn't just move so that she could, but got out of bed to help her. Between her legs was sore, and she winced twice when sliding her legs off the bed. Telling him she was sore, she touched the top of her head too and felt the tenderness of her scalp. "I'm sore. Very much so. And so you know, I've never wanted that kind of sex before, and I loved it."

He helped her to the bathroom, and when she was finished, she decided to take a shower. Amber wasn't sure she was going to be able to move to clean herself up, so she was glad that Guy joined her. He took the nice sponge from her and filled it with the soap that was on the top of the tile.

"I don't know that I'd want to order you around like that again because it took a lot out of me to do it. But I really enjoyed it as well." He washed her hair back then, her hair while she stood under the hot spray. "I've fallen in love with you, Amber. I don't know when, but while I watched you sleep, I realized that I think I've been in love with you since the first time I saw you at the bank."

After rinsing her hair, she turned to look at him. While he did look a great deal like his brothers, there was something so natural about him. He didn't comb his hair in any fancy way—none of them did that, but he just seemed to run his fingers through it, and that was the end of his grooming. He could look dressed up, she was sure, but she loved the way that he just looked like he stepped out of the shower with her.

"I'm falling in love with you as well. I don't know why, you've been a brute, but I am falling for you." He promised her that he'd change his ways so that she could be someone that she could be proud of. "I don't want you to change for me. I want you to change for you and only if you want to. I can live with the brute now that I know what you said to me. I do love you, Guy. Very much so."

They kissed, a long, lingering one, then she washed his back and chest. She couldn't do his hair as he'd done to hers because he was taller than her. But she did enjoy running the sponge over his chest when they were playing around.

"No more sex today." He laughed, then smiled at her. Telling her that he didn't think he could go another round right now had her laughing. The place on her neck where he'd bitten her was tender and a little sore, but she knew too that he'd marked her as his and that was fine by her. She was in love with Guy, and she wanted the whole world to know it.

She was feeling better after the shower. In fact, the two of them made the bed together, and she got to ask him about the mattress. He told her that he was a big guy and had found this larger than life bed and had a mattress made for it.

"It fits my body and there is plenty enough room for you too." She hadn't felt crowded in the bed now that he'd mentioned it. "I've only had it for about a week, and now that you're going to be sharing a bed with me, I think it's perfect."

Breakfast was only cereal and toast. She didn't have to get up and make hers because Guy was being the perfect gentleman. As they talked about their day, she told him that she really needed to go to the bank and set herself up an account so that she could get to some money. He told her that he'd put her name on his accounts, and if she wanted to put her money in that account, he'd not bother it.

"I like that we'll share an account. We can share bills too. My parents used to pay something from their own accounts. My dad paid the mortgage, and my mom would pay the electric. It worked out well for them, but if either of them went over one month, they'd have to borrow it from the other person and pay them back. I always thought that was silly. Two people should share the same account and bills. Is that all right with you?" He told her that as far as he knew, his parents never paid bills, so whatever she set up, he'd be fine with it. "All right. Also, the money that you gave me to lend to my brother. I'll pay you back."

"You just said we'd share bills. As far as I'm concerned, all that I have is yours, and all that you have is yours as well. I rarely spend money on myself, but I have been spending money on the house. I love how it makes me feel to have new things around me. They don't have to be modern, just new to me. I love having things that make us comfortable."

After breakfast, they cleaned up the little bit of mess they'd made and made their way to the bank. Guy drove his car there as it had gotten colder overnight, and there was about six more inches of snow on the ground. While out and about, they decided to get some groceries as well as a few things for the bedroom that they now shared. She needed her own shampoo and body wash, and it was exciting for her to smell the scents with Guy to have him pick out the one he liked the most.

~*~

Guy felt better than he had in weeks, more like years. As they were shopping, he kept his eyes out for not just her family but his as well. Not that he'd avoid his own family, but they were having fun just being a couple, and he didn't want anyone to intrude on their time together. He knew as soon as he got back to the house, he was going to have to work again, and he didn't mind it so much. It was fun again, writing instead of him sneaking away to hide from his housemate.

The book was going better than he thought that any had before. The words just seemed to flow onto the page, and he liked that when he read back over it, there were few mistakes—like none that he could find. He knew that he was looking at it with fresh eyes and would miss a few things, but that's what he had a wonderful editor for. To make him shine.

Paying for the cartload of things that they found, Guy didn't even look at the sales slip when it was put into the bag. He was feeling too right with the world to make a big deal out of anything so trivial as something small rung up incorrectly. When they were headed to the door, he saw his brother Edmond. There was no avoiding him once he saw them.

"I was just coming to see you." Guy told him no. "No, you don't want me to come to visit?" He seemed to be dense, and it was Amber who clued him into them wanting to get to know one another better. "I see. But I do have something that I'd like to run by you. I promise it'll be quick. It's about your staff."

"We need to run anyone by Brandy so that she

can do a background check." He nodded as if he knew that. "Do you have someone in mind? We need a cook first and foremost."

"This will work out perfectly. One of the women that we've been asked to set up a new life for has requested to be a house worker." Edmond laughed. "When we started this underground thing with getting people out, I never once thought of someone coming here to hide out. Anyway, Brandy has done the background check on her, and other than a jaywalking ticket some years ago, she's clean. Can I send her over so that the two of you can interview her? Her name is Allison Wears. She's an older woman who is running from her children, who think that she needs to be a full-time sitter. They think that she went to visit her sister and that will be the last time she returns to them."

"We need a cook, so that's fine. But don't come over today. In fact, tell the others not to come over either. We're getting to know each other, and I don't want to have to put up with you guys while we're at it." Edmond nodded and smiled that knowing smile while he stood there. "I'm serious. Go away, Edmond. I have better things to do than to stand around and talk about you for the rest of the day."

"I'm going. I'm happy for you both." He could more than likely smell on them that they'd bonded, but he wouldn't know how much fun they'd had at it. Or perhaps he did, being that he was newly mated as well. "I'll send Allison over in the morning. That should be enough time for you to get some supplies into your home so that she can start right away. If not, then you'll have supplies for when you huddle down in your home."

After he left, they left as well. Once home, it took them two trips each for them to get all the things in the house that they'd purchased. That wasn't even counting the supplies like flour and other kitchen things they needed to order and have delivered. He didn't want to go out into the weather again.

Getting things put away was going to be Amber's job, as he really did need to get onto the book. The need to write it was something that he experienced every time he worked on a book, and this one was no different. As soon as he was able to sit down, it was like he plugged back into the book and began writing. It didn't bother him that before leaving the computer earlier in the day he'd left in mid-sentence. He just picked it up like he never left the room.

At a quarter to six, he was finished for the day. He went in search of Amber. She was in the living room taking a nap, and he didn't have the heart to wake her. So, sitting across from her on the other couch, he watched her sleep. It was the most calming thing that he'd ever done, and he loved it. After about an hour of just watching her sleep, he decided that he would go and fix them some dinner. Not knowing what they had made it an adventure for him, one that he was excited to try. But his plans were off when he encountered someone in the kitchen cooking something that smelled delicious.

"The missus called your brother and had me come over. Then the two of us set up an order to be brought in. I hope you don't mind." He said that if whatever she was cooking was for their dinner, he didn't mind at all. "Yes. Got some pork chops simmering on the stove with some green beans and corn to be as the side. Since I was getting a late start, you won't have any rolls or bread that's fresh, but I'll have it tomorrow for you. Do you have anything that you won't eat? The missus said she doesn't eat broccoli."

Broccoli is one of my favorite vegetables, so I'll eat her portion." She laughed with him, and it occurred to him that it felt good to laugh with a stranger. "Like my family, we eat a lot of meat, with the exception of my brother Ayden. He will not eat red meat at all. But I'll eat just about anything that you serve me. If I don't, well then I'll let you know if I don't like something."

"Good. I would hate to have served you something that you don't enjoy. I love to cook. Kinda got out of the habit when my kids were forever dropping off their kids and leaving them with me for days on end. Got sick of having to shell out money to do it for them, too. Awful children. Nowadays, I guess, a lot of grandparents are raising their grandkids. Well, I put my foot down. They all work and can afford things that I can't, so I just left them to it. Better than saying I don't want to babysit anymore."

"We've only been together for a short time, so I don't know if we want kids or not." He didn't know why he told her that and was embarrassed when she seemed to be. That was when he realized that she was a wolf too. "You've met my brother, Lica, I take it. He's the pack alpha."

"I have. Powerfully nice man if you ask me. All of you Fraizer men are, too." That made him proud that she didn't single him out for not being nice. He felt good, too, that he was able to have a conversation with her and not have her pissed off. Must be Amber's influence was all he could think about.

Eating in the dining room seemed over the top, so the two of them ate in the kitchen with Katy. She told them stories about her old life as a grannie babysitter, and he told her what he did for a living. Amber was looking for a job that she could do that would fulfill her, and he was happy for her. She didn't want to be a stay-at-home housewife, and he didn't blame her. The four walls of the house could really get to a person after a while, and he knew that for sure. Plus, there was also the added bonus of being able to be ready for her when she did come home from work. That appealed to him a great deal.

After dinner, the two of them went to the living room and talked. There was no topic that was too embarrassing, and they had a wonderful time. Amber did want children, and he was glad. He could see the halls of his home filled with laughter and fun, and that excited him a great deal. Also, to see her fat with his child was something that he never thought of before, a woman having his children.

Chapter 7

Amber was running behind. Again. Every time she would ask Guy about the outfit she had on, he would try to take it off her. The man was insatiable. And she loved every minute of it. Finally locking him out of the bedroom, she was able to get dressed without his help, and now she was running behind. Not by much, but it could have been worse. She was shown to their table as soon as she showed up for the lunch date with the other women in the family.

"I'm so glad you could make it on such short notice. I've been meaning to call you all week, but things just kept getting in the way. Mostly Lica, but we're getting that taken care of, too." She felt her face heat up when she wondered if it was the same reason she was late, but let it go. "Do you have a job yet? Guy said that you were looking for something part-time."

"I don't want to be gone all day and have to come home exhausted. We're getting the house set up the way that we want it, and I think that we're having too much fun just being a couple for a change." She decided that was too much information and changed the subject back to the original question. "No, I've not found anything as yet. I did apply at a couple of places in town, but was told that if I wanted to take jobs from the poor, I should move to the next town. Not too friendly around here about the Fraizers, are people?"

"Mr. Jenkins, I'm betting." Summer nodded when she did. "He's in big trouble with the Feds. He was audited just a few days ago, and we're all waiting for the results to come back. He was charging fifty percent more in the way of taxes to any shifter in town, especially to the wolves. Then he didn't report the extra income on his taxes. He's going to prison if I don't miss my bet."

"He was the one. Even told me I wasn't allowed to shop in his store because I might sully it up. Whatever. I can find the things he has in his store online for much cheaper. Thanks for letting me know about him. I'll avoid him in the future." She reached for one of the rolls that had been set on the table. "I'm starving. It's been forever since breakfast, I feel like."

"I am as well. I ordered a few appetizers for the table, so they should be coming soon. By the way, is there anything you don't eat? Sometimes when we're all together, I cater the food so that I don't have to cook." Mac teased her about ordering food out all the time if she didn't have a cook. "I know I should take more time to cook meals, but I'm so busy running my grandma's business. It's fun, but I think I'm ready to turn it over to someone else to mess with. I think that — that's what I wanted to talk to you about. I have a part-time job for you to do if you want it. Guy said you could do books. I have two little companies that don't have a bookkeeper, and you'd be perfect. You can even do it from your house as they're that small."

"That sounds right up my alley. I'd love to do that." They talked for a few minutes about what the job would entail and how much it paid, just as the appetizers arrived. She took one of the deep-fried cheese sticks and a ravioli. They were both hot, but she didn't care; she really was very hungry. "Burning off energy is hard work when you're with one of the Frazier men, isn't it?"

She couldn't believe that she said that and was embarrassed when they all three agreed with her. She supposed there was a lot to be said for marrying brothers, and she knew these women were very outspoken about a lot of things. Amber would have to be careful in the future in case she said something very revealing.

They did talk about anything and everything. There were topics about babies, Brandy having the little one at home, and they spoke about the upcoming pack meeting that was going to introduce the new members of the family. Guy had told her about that, and she was happy to get to know the other members of the pack that she was now a part of. By the time they had ordered their food and it was brought to them, she thought that they had exhausted every subject that could be talked about.

"Now we get down to business. There are some people coming in through our network who are going to need jobs. Guy and Amber have already hired one of them, but there are four more that are needed to have a place to work." She knew this topic was going to come up and had been prepared for it. She told them about the job that still needed to be filled at the slaughterhouse. Plus, she and Guy were going to need someone to come in once a day to clean up the house for them.

"We're not messy by any means of the word, but it would be nice to come home to clean bathrooms and bedrooms. Cleaning around Guy is hard enough. He gets to writing, and there is no disturbing him with vacuuming or dusting." They all agreed that having someone in the house to do those things was really nice. "I don't, however, know if I could employ someone full-time, and I'm betting that's what they're looking for."

"Getting them into the workforce is more important than how many hours they'll be working. I know for a fact that two of the people who were brought in have been out of work for a while, so anything would be good for them. The male in the group can work at the slaughterhouse with the others. And either one of the women, though I think that the job is a little strenuous for one of the women, she's nothing but a twig, but I could be wrong about her. She might do better than the men who work there." They all laughed, and then the spotlight was turned to her. "You said not full-time, but I'm betting that having someone in the house is going to make you want her full-time. She can make up the beds and dust things, but she can also wash windows and things like that. I've seen your home, don't forget, and it has a lot of windows that look out over the yard. I'm betting that by spring, you'll need yard work as well. We have someone who mows and trims. By the time he's finished up with the yard, it's time to start all over again. He does make us look good with the flowers and bushes being trimmed up as well."

After the lunch plates were taken away, they decided that they needed dessert. She'd never been a big fan of sweets, not like Guy was, but she did order herself some fruit. She thought that she could eat that for every meal that she had. Just as she was finishing up, she got a call from the doctor who was monitoring Margaret.

"She's run off again." She asked him how many times she'd done it so far. "This is the third time. She's usually in the same place, back at the house I was made to understand was yours. Thank goodness the police found her this time. I don't know what to do about this. I don't even know why she ends up there."

Amber had an idea that it was to hurt her, but didn't say anything to the doctor. He did tell her that he was going to have to hire more help if she was going to continue this way, and she agreed with him. He also asked her about her brother, who Margaret seems to focus on a great deal.

"He's working a full-time job, and I guess she might be missing him." She'd also heard that he wasn't working out so well at the house. Instead of working like he was supposed to, he was hanging around the others and watching them. Lica was going to fire him soon if he didn't get his crap together. "I know that he lives there with her, too. Maybe she misses him, like I said. Could be, couldn't it?"

"I would say that if he'd never had a job before, now that she more than likely has become dependent on him when he was around. Neither one of them has worked very much, have they? Neither one of them has a good grasp on money either." She agreed with him. "Well, I just wanted to let you know about her running off again and to tell you that I'm nearly finished with my evaluation. I don't know what you expected from this, but I'm sure it's going to be bringing some hard truths about the two of them. I'm glad you told me to see about his, Mr. Gross's, interaction with his sister. I think them to be an odd pair if you want to know the truth of it."

She smiled at his wording and wondered if he'd put that in the report to her and Guy. She and Guy had been talking a great deal about her family. Belinda, too, had some input on the matter and told Guy to tell her not to be alone with either of them. They were not just an odd pair, but they were also dangerous. Just how dangerous was the question.

Still thinking about her brother, she asked Brandy, while they were getting ready to leave, if she could talk to her. After telling her everything she knew about Shawn and Margaret, including the fact that they killed their parents, she asked her if she wanted to see them go to jail. It was already a cold case and would go on being one, it looked to her like.

"He's fucking up at work." Brandy nodded as if she knew that already. And she more than likely did with living with Lica. "Belinda, my stepmother said not to trust either one of them. I agree with her, but don't know what to do about them getting away with murder."

"Yes, you do. You just don't want to be the one who pulls the police in on the matter." She started to deny that, but realized that she was right. He'd been trying, which was the last conversation she'd had with him, and now to find out that he wasn't even trying hurt her a bit. "I can help you in any way that you wish. I can have them put in jail on suspicion of murder, and we can figure out what the courts have to say about it. I was told that there was a film of them murdering their mother. It wouldn't take anything at all to clean that up so that it's clear as crystal for the police."

"I think I need to talk to Guy." Brandy said that he would help her see what she wanted to do. "I know. He keeps telling me that he'll go along with whatever I want, but I don't think he cares for the fact that there are two murderers just out free to do what they want while two other people are dead."

"To be honest with you, Amber, that's the way I feel, too. They've literally gotten away with murder, and no one seems to be bringing that up. Or caring for that matter." She said that she did, but didn't know what to do then. "But you do now, correct?"

"Yes, they need to be held accountable for their actions. Yes, that's what I want to do." Nodding, feeling the burden being taken off her shoulders, they hugged. "You're a good friend, Brandy. Thank you for talking to me about this."

"You knew what you were going to do before we spoke. You just needed someone to vent to. I know what you mean about Guy telling you it's your decision, but I want you to know that he fully believes that. Any one of the men would walk the earth for you, but they'd never put you in a position where you have to be the heavy on something alone. They'd be right there by your side." She agreed with her again and hugged her a second time. "You give great hugs. Has anyone told you that before?"

"No. I wasn't much of a hugger until recently. It's like an affirmation on friendship to me. I find that I feel so much better about things when I've had the contact of a good friend like that." Brandy thanked her. "No need for that. You have become a good friend to me and the others as well. I think that's what Guy and I both needed. Friendship with his family."

Amber was glad that she'd walked to the restaurant. It had put her more behind, but the day was a good seventy degrees outside, and she had herself a new coat and boots for all the melting snow. They were predicting more snow tomorrow, so she wanted to enjoy the weather while it was here. Just as she was going into the house, Guy opened the door for her.

"Don't panic." She said that she hated that statement. "I don't blame you, but I don't want you to freak out, and that one is even worse than not to panic. Anyway, your sister has been arrested. She tried to break into your home and was found to have a gun." Guy pulled her into the house and held her as they continued the conversation.

"She was looking for me. Correct?" He said that she wasn't talking yet, so he hadn't heard. "What other reason would she need a gun at my home other than to cause me harm. I'm going to press charges this time. Has Shawn been notified?"

"He's been fired from his job. Lica went over to talk to him, and he was sleeping on the desk in the office. He said to tell you he was sorry, but he'd had enough." Good, she told Guy and said she'd tell Lica that as well. "I thought you'd say that. I also have news on the murder of Belinda. The video has been cleaned up, and it shows the two of them with the baseball bat, both before and after they hit her in the head with it. The reason that the two kids were able to do it is because they hit her a total of eleven times. Five and six times each. The officer who was talking to me said they danced around and laughed; it looked like to him, after they'd done the deed. They'll be arresting Shawn as soon as they find him."

"He's missing?" He told her what he knew. "Oh. I never thought of the car being taken from him when he got fired. I hate that he was hired on my recommendation, but at least he'll be going to jail too."

Amber told Guy everything that she'd talked to the doctor about, as well as the conversation that she'd had with Brandy after the lunch. She also told him about the woman who had been hired to keep their home nice. He was all right with everything she'd said to him.

"I don't know what to feel right now." He said that he was in the same boat. Glad it was over with so far, and upset at how easily it went down. "They've not caught Shawn yet, so we don't want that to jinx that for the police." The knock at the door startled them both.

Guy turned his back to the door and looked at her. *"Don't move. Not even if it looks like things are going well."* She nodded. *"Stay behind me and don't move. I can't stand the fact that I might lose you...it's your brother, and while I can't smell the gun on him, he's been someplace where someone or him fired one. Also, I've called in my brothers. They're on their way here now."*

"All right." She moved back from the door and Guy in the event he needed to shift. While she'd never seen his wolf, she had heard that he was bigger than a normal-sized wolf and more dangerous. *"Be careful and stay safe."*

"I promise I will be better at taking him on if I don't have to worry about you." He opened the door and asked her brother what he wanted. Shawn asked if she was here.

"She's here. I'm sure you saw her coming home just now. I believe that she's in the kitchen." Amber backed away from the wall and slipped into the closet.

She didn't know what her brother would do right now, but she didn't want to be in the way if he had to be killed. And that, she thought, was what she was hoping for. "What can I do for you?"

"Your brother fired me." He asked him what he'd done. "Why do you think that I did anything wrong? Maybe he's the one that fucked up by firing me. I was doing a good job there."

"No, you weren't. You were sleeping on the job when he found you." He asked him where he'd heard that from. "My brother. He said that it wasn't the first time that you've been caught sleeping on the job, either."

"It was a shitty job anyway. Who wants to smell like meat all the time? Where's my sister, Amber? Don't think I didn't notice that you didn't tell me where she was." He said he'd told him she was in the kitchen. "Well, I want to talk to her about this. We have more bills coming in all the time, and they're not getting paid. I don't have a job anymore, so Amber is going to have to fork over some more money soon, or we'll be out of everything."

"I'm thinking that you should have thought of that when you were sleeping on the job. Bills are out there for everyone. And they need to be paid. Having a job and keeping one is the only way that they're going to get paid." He said that Amber needed to help them again. "I don't think that's going to happen."

Just as she was snuggling herself back more in the closet, she heard Guy laugh as he asked Shawn what he was going to do with the gun he had. That scared her, but she stayed where she was. There was no point in her getting hurt when she had a wolf to take care of her.

"I told you that I want to speak to my sister, Amber. You're to bring her to me right now." Guy told him no and said that she was safe where she was. "Well, that's not going to work for me right now. I know that they arrested Margaret. Why the hell is Amber staying around here instead of at the house that she got from her mom? Margaret's been watching for her, but that doctor keeps finding her and bringing her back."

That scared her more than just the gun being pointed at Guy. They'd been stalking her. Not only that, but she'd bet anything that Margaret would have killed her given the chance. Staying where she was, she was nervous for Guy. If Shawn had a gun, then that meant that he was pointing it directly at her mate. When the gun went off, she felt a tightness in the air around her and then nothing.

"*Don't come out here.*" She said she wouldn't, then asked if he was dead. "*He is. There is no point in you seeing this. Also, I've been shot. In the left shoulder.*"

"*Let me come out and see you. Better yet, you come*

to me." He said that he was his wolf so that when he shifted back, he'd be healed. She was better off where she was for the police. *"All right, but I don't like it."*

"Neither do I that I had to kill him. My brothers are here. Ivan said that it's a clean shot in and out. Also, Devlin is here in the event I get arrested. I might. But we'll have to wait on the police to see. They're just pulling into the driveway now." She felt stupid being in the closet, but figured that he was right; she was better off there than fussing at Guy. When she heard the sirens, she felt marginally better. *"I love you, Guy."*

"And I love you. Not too much longer now, and we'll be able to be at home safe again." She liked that idea. Being safe anywhere was a good thing.

~*~

They did arrest him, which he figured they would. Amber was finally able to come out of the closet, for which he was grateful for. She could see him now, and she did fuss, but he loved it. It was nice being pampered again, but by her this time instead of the children. As he was being pulled away, he asked about Margaret.

"Her doctor came and got her. We have the gun. They must have each had one, and we're going to be running tests on them to see if either one of them killed their father. The video was cleaned up about the murder of Belinda Gross, and I'd never have believed it if I didn't see it with my own eyes. Them kids, they were just kids, too, killed her where she was standing like she was nothing more than a bubble they were popping in the air." Apt description, he thought, since they had bashed her skull in. "We're going out to the house to do a search and to arrest Margaret. Glad to have these two cases off the books, I tell you what."

"I bet you are." Guy was put in a cell but was told he'd not be there too long. They knew it was justified for him to kill Shawn. "When my wife gets here, will you allow her to come back and see me, John? This has been kinda hard on her, knowing that her family killed her dad and stepmom."

"She'll be able to if I have to bring her back myself." He felt better about that and was soon told that she and his attorney were there. Devlin told him not to say anything when he left, and the police seemed to understand that. None of them had asked him a single question about the way things went down. "You write me up something when your brother gets here, can't you, Guy? For our own records."

"Whatever Devlin says. You know I always trust him." John told him that it was good to have an attorney around all the time and left him to his cell. As soon as he saw Amber, her crying about how she didn't like this at all, Guy told her how much he loved her. She seemed to calm down a bit when she saw that his shoulder was completely healed and he wasn't covered in blood. Yes, he thought, he could get used to this pampering a bit more.

When Devlin okayed for him to write out a statement, he was told not to tell anyone that he shifted to take care of himself. Everyone would understand, no doubt, but if someone who didn't know what was going on got hold of the paperwork, they'd not understand. The next thing he was told was that Margaret was dead as well. Killed by police.

"We were set to arrest her when she pulled out another gun. They must have gotten a discount on them, that's all I can figure out. Well, she pulled it out and shot her doctor. Then the nurse who was set to work with him. When she fired into my men, they opened fire on her and killed her right off. Thing is, she kept asking where her brother was, and we'd told her right off that he was dead." Guy did tell them that she had trouble with simple things and wouldn't listen to things that she didn't want to hear. "That sounds about right. She was fixated on the fact that he'd not been with us when we came to pick her up. This one is for the books, I tell you what."

After writing his statement out and letting his brother read it over, he was set free to leave. John, of course, told him not to leave town, and he said that he'd not. Not that they'd care if he went to Columbus so long as he promised them he'd come back home.

That's the sort of thing you got in small towns, trust.

He was suddenly exhausted when he returned home. Dozing on the couch with Amber, he told her in bits and pieces how his book was going. It wasn't until he got up to get himself something to snack on that he noticed that Belinda was gone. Calling out for her brought her to him, but she looked oddly ghostlike more than before.

"I'm moving on. I just wanted to make sure that Amber got her money and my death was solved." He told her that he was going to miss her. "And I'll miss you too, you big lug."

She looked around the room they were in, then she stared at him. Telling him to take care of Amber while he was still on this earthly plane. Guy promised that he would for the rest of his life and that he'd name his first daughter after her.

"Don't do that. Belinda isn't a name that I ever liked." He said that he did and that if Amber was willing, they'd be having them a little Belinda in the house chasing after ghosts if she wanted. "All right, that'll be nice. Maybe her grandpa and I will come to visit her when you least expect it. That'll be nice, won't it? For us to come around to see the little girl. If you have one?"

"You bet it would." He said he wished that he could hug her. "I was never much into hugs until I met your Amber; now it's all I can do not to hug everyone I come across."

"You just take care of her while you're living, and I'll not have to come back here and kick your ass. And just so you know, I can do that." They both laughed, and Amber joined them in the room. "I was just telling your mate here to take care of you, but you'd better be taking care of him, too. He's a better man since he got his head out of his ass and started living again." Guy told her what she'd said to her.

"I'm going to take care of both of us." She nodded and looked so sad for a moment. "I wish you didn't have to go. I know whatever brought you here is finished, but I'm going to miss being able to talk to you through Guy."

"I'll be back when that book hits the bestseller list. You dedicate it to me, and I'll promise not to tell anyone the ending before they get the chance to read it. You telling them that a ghost helped you write your masterpiece?" Guy laughed and said that he did, but she was the only one that he'd see in the future, too. "That's too bad. You do well with the unliving."

Again, they both laughed, and Belinda started to fade away. When she was nearly gone, she came back and kissed him on the cheek. He didn't feel anything, of course, but he loved that she'd done that to him. Then she was gone in a puff of smoke like magic.

After getting something to eat, the two of them went up to bed. He was tired, and he knew that Amber was as well. With so much stress lifted off their shoulders, he felt like he could sleep for a month and not get enough. Amber told him that she had an appointment in the morning with the two places that she was going to be working with, so that's where she'd be if he woke up and she was gone.

It didn't take them long to get settled into the bed. Even before the light was out, he was nearly asleep. When he wrapped himself around Amber and pulled her close to his body, he felt his mind shutting down to all things that had been running in there hourly, and went to sleep. Tomorrow was going to be a long day of writing, he knew that and was looking forward to it more than he had recently.

He woke once in the middle of the night, at least it was still dark outside, and went to the bathroom. On his way back, he looked at his phone and couldn't believe that it was just after two in the morning. Going back to bed, he thought he'd be awake for a while, but as soon as his head hit the pillow, he was out again.

The next time he woke up, he couldn't believe how good he felt. It wasn't until he looked at his phone again to find the time that he realized that he'd slept for nearly twenty hours. He must have needed it because he felt wonderful. Getting up to get cleaned up, he reached out for Amber to tell her that he was finally awake. She laughed.

"I wondered if you were going to sleep around the clock. I've been up for hours." He told her he was sorry. *"Don't be. You must have needed it, or I'd have been able to wake you up the few times that I tried. I love you, Guy, and come down when you're ready. We're having subs for dinner since I didn't know when you'd wake."*

He told her that he would and still felt good. After his shower, he met her in the kitchen and kissed her fully on the mouth. This was just what he needed. A good night's sleep, a woman, and food, he told her. She asked him if it had to be in that order, and that made him laugh too.

Chapter 8

Ivan looked at the little dog and then at the three bite marks on his hand. Why he wasn't cooperating was beyond him, but the little shit didn't want to be examined, and that was making him fight with him. The little shit was driving him crazy.

"He bites me all the time." He wanted to ask Debbie why she kept the shit if he was forever biting her. "Mom said since I wanted him, I have to deal with all that comes with him. I just want to toss him in front of a car and be done with him, Doc Ivan. I won't do that, but some days it's hard not to."

"I understand, honey. But I can't examine him if he's like this. I'm going to have to sedate him again." The last time he'd done that, he'd found out the shit had worms. Maybe he liked having them full in his belly. "Mom give you permission for me to do that again?"

"She said he's my responsibility. Will he calm down enough for you to see if he needs any more medicine?" He wanted to tell her they could ship him away if she wanted, but didn't think that was going to go over too well with the mom. Debbie might be all right with it, but he doubted that he'd get any repeat business for disappearing dogs. "I don't care what you do to him so long as he stops biting me. Last week I had to have three stitches to fix my ankle, and he tore up my shoes too. On top of that, my mom grounded me because he ate one of her shoes too. I hate this dog."

It took him ten minutes to sedate the shit. Even then, he seemed to be snapping and biting at something in his dreams. After giving him a thorough examination, he decided that enough was enough. He was going to have to say something to the mother. The dog wasn't fit for apartment dwelling. He needed to be on a large farm where hopefully something bigger than him would eat him. At the very least, teach it some manners.

Mom wasn't thrilled about his advice that the dog was too anxious for an apartment, that he might need to go to some open spaces, a farm perhaps. She told him that she, too, hated the dog, and all he would do was wonder why they were keeping him. While he didn't condone swapping out dogs for something better, this case was a danger to everyone in the household, including him. He said he'd ask around to see what he could find.

"Good. I didn't think that Debbie was old enough to have a dog anyway. Maybe this will teach her a lesson in that mother knows best." He did wonder if the mother had picked out this dog to be with her daughter to 'teach her a lesson'. But he wasn't sure. That seemed to be the norm for this woman. "You let me know if you find someone. I'm not going to take the dog there; they'll have to come and get him. Just getting him in the car was bad enough to come here. I had to allow Debbie to get bitten again."

Mother of the year, he thought, but didn't so much as look at her. As he was putting the dog into his cage, he mentally reached out to one of his brothers that were working at the slaughterhouse today. Maybe there was enough land for the stupid dog to get out where he should have been all along.

"Bring him out. I don't have time to go and pick him up. Is this the little dog that bit Debbie Lane the other day? Her mom brought her into the hospital while I was there getting information on the deaths of Shawn and Margaret." Ivan told Guy that it was the one. *"Figures. The mother was bitching to the little girl about making the dog bite her. There are just some dogs that can not be trained. That one is one of them. Bring him out, and he can roam around here with the other dogs. Maybe he might learn something from them, who knows?"*

"Since he's already in the cage, perhaps she won't mind dropping him off. I'll see and let you know. But I'd not take him out unless he's sedated. He's a mean little shit. I

was bitten by him three times just today." Guy asked if it was the child. *"I don't think she's doing anything to him. I know she was excited to train him, but she told me today that she hates him. I think a lot of that has to do with the mom. She seems bent on blaming the little girl for everything about the dog."*

Mrs. Lane wasn't happy about taking the dog to the farm, but in the end, he told her that he'd have to have another appointment to sedate him to get him out of the cage if she didn't take him today. Debbie seemed so relieved to be getting the dog out of her life that he was worried she'd never have a pet again. That would be a shame. Pets and children go together. So long as there is support at home.

The rest of the afternoon and into the evening were just appointments. He did see a cat today, who didn't care for a wolf taking care of her, but she settled down in the end. The dogs usually never had any trouble with him taking care of them, and he did wonder about the Lane dog. He hoped he would do well at the farm and knew that he could check on the little shit while he was out there, too.

It was snowing again when he left work, and he made his way over to see Guy. He wanted him to look at something at the house, and he was more than willing to stop by. They would invite him to dinner, and he loved eating at the big house. It was the nicest one of all his brothers' with wives homes. Their cook usually served up the best meals, too. Better than he could make himself at his home.

Ivan loved his new home. It was large enough that he could get lost in it if he wanted. Just yesterday, he was in the upstairs bedrooms measuring and had missed a salesman coming to his door. It was perfectly large enough for that. Plus, he was sleeping better than he had when they'd all been living on the farm. It was nice too to know that it was all his.

"Come on in. I have a couple of things going on in the kitchen. Want to join me?" He told Amber that he would love to join her in his favorite part of the house. "Guy says that the kitchen is his favorite part, too. He calls it the heart of the home. We're working on making this a home."

"What have you got going on? Maybe I can help you before Guy gets here." She told him that she'd gotten a table and chairs at the market the other day and thought now that it was too big for the space she wanted to put it in. "You want to eat in the kitchen?"

"It's easier on the staff if we don't mess up the dining room. Besides, it's so big we have to have something that we can talk to each other in while we're dining in it. I love the room, don't get me wrong. When it's only the two of us, it's just too much work." She showed him the table and the space she had. "I hope we can get it to work. I love this old table, and the chairs are very comfortable."

Not only did they get it to work by taking out one of the leaves, but they were able to put the four chairs around it. Ivan said he'd not mind eating in the kitchen when asked and told Amber he was hoping for an invite to dinner.

"Yes, please stay and have a meal with us. Since Belinda has moved on, the house is kind of quiet. Not that I could speak to her or anything, but she and Guy had a lot of conversations. Did he tell you that he's almost finished with the book? I think that's why he wanted you to come over. He's having trouble with the cover samples that he'd been sent. I don't care for either of them, but then I'm not writing the book."

"I've helped him before. I don't have any trouble telling him that I don't care for the cover or not. Once he decided to use a cover that I vetoed, he had to change it out because there were complaints about it. I think it was the font that was too difficult to read or something like that." Guy wasn't due for another half hour, so they had some veggies on a platter with dip to hold them off. "I didn't get a lunch today, and it's beginning to show on my wolf. He hates when I skip meals."

"I'm trying to get into the habit of eating all three meals here. When Guy isn't home or busy, I forget to get me something for the noonday meal. It's not that big of a deal, I can usually get something light for snacking before dinner, but I get the worst kind of headaches when I skip lunch." She laughed, and Ivan loved to hear it. "What will you do when your mate comes along, Ivan? Have you got your house in order?"

"Not even close. I've been buying things to fill it out, but the trouble is I don't have any furniture in most of the rooms. I have a couple of air mattresses in some of the rooms, but nothing more than that. I've been waiting on spring so that I can hit up a couple of auctions." She said that was what Guy was excited to do. "I didn't know you guys didn't have your house done."

"We do for the most part, but like you, we don't have much in the way of furniture for the bedrooms. Ours, of course, is done, but there are still six more that need to have something in them. I'm looking for a bunkbed set to set up in one of the rooms in the event some of the nieces want to stay over. They just love Guy to pieces." He said they'd make it a day when the weather got better. "Yes, I heard the weather is going to turn nasty again tomorrow. I hope not. I have a couple of places that I have to be in the afternoon."

"I'll take you if it gets really bad. I close up the clinic when the weather is at its worst. The people don't want to risk their pets coming all the way in for just a checkup." He laughed a little and told her about the dog he'd had today. "I've been dealing with him because of Debbie, but her mom has her so stressed out about the mutt that she hates it. I can see that too. Her mom is something else."

By the time Guy made it home, it had started to snow again. They were predicting that they could get as much as six more inches on the stuff they had already. She was making plans to not have to go into town tomorrow by the time they sat down to dinner. Ivan had already closed up the clinic due to the bad weather.

Dinner was fantastic. Just the right kind of food for a cold night. He loved chili and cornbread together and thought that the cook had made it perfectly sweet, too. As he was eating the last bite of his cherry crunch, Guy showed him the covers that he was working with.

"I don't like either of them." He picked them both up and put them on the wall with some tape. "I don't like them even when they're far away. Your editor or whoever must really like that font. It's the same one from before that you got complaints about, isn't it?" Guy said that he thought it was now that he pointed it out to him. "I'd just tell him to back off from it. It doesn't work."

"I will when I tell him about these. I was hoping for more in line with the other books I've written, but he said it would mess up the genre. I don't know, I've written books before that weren't murder mysteries." He laughed a little. "I might need to have my publisher find me someone else to edit. I don't even know why he's making my covers. For all I know, he could be just taking this on himself."

"I'd bet that's what's going on. I'm glad you trust my opinion, too." They sat in the living room, and the fireplace was roaring out the heat. "I think I could take a nap for about two days right now. My belly is full, and it's warm in here. Perfect night for it too."

"You should spend the night. Even though I told you that the bedrooms aren't finished, one of them is. It has a beautiful view of the yard out back, and I love that there's a gas fireplace in there, too. That one is going to be popular when the kids come to sleep over." Guy agreed with Amber about his spending the night. "I'll feel safer about you not driving home in this if you just stay here. You don't have any plans for tomorrow anyway, and you can hang out with me."

"I'd love that if you're sure you don't mind." He was concerned about the roads and was happy for the invite. As all his brothers did, he had an extra set of clothing in his car and ran out to get it before the snow started piling up. Coming back into the house, he told them that if the weather doesn't change soon, he might be spending the week here. "The snow is hard, too, not that fluffy white stuff we had before."

Since he was staying the night, he didn't bother them and went up to bed at about nine-thirty. His room was very nice, and after getting the fireplace going, it turned into a nice toasty room for himself too. Getting into bed because he really was feeling the effects of the food and warmth, Ivan picked up one of Guy's books he'd given him and started reading. He knew it was a mistake to start on it when it was nearly two in the morning, before he could put it down. His brother could really write like a master.

After getting a shower the next morning, he was glad again that he had spent the night. The snow was coming down harder today than last night, and his car was covered. The driveway looked impassible, and he was glad that Guy had walked into town rather than driving. It wasn't that cold, about thirty degrees, but the snow was wet now and stuck to you like glue when you were out in it. He was happy that his brother had a snow blower when he asked if he could plow the driveway for them.

It was more fun than he thought it should have been plowing the driveway. The snow was being tossed about ten feet into the air, and it landed just outside the driveway. While he was at it, he even did the sidewalks and in front of the mailbox. He was going to have to get himself one of these things, he thought, and was happy that he'd been able to test drive Guy's.

Coming into the house, Amber had made sure that he had plenty of towels and hot cocoa. He didn't care for marshmallows in it, but he didn't want to hurt her feelings. She'd gone to a lot of trouble having him spend the night, and now this. He really liked his newest sister-in-law and thought that she and Guy made about the most perfect couple. His brother sure was different since he'd met her and wondered, not for the first time, what kind of changes would happen to him when he finally met his mate.

Ivan wasn't opposed to meeting his mate. In fact, he thought it was the most exciting thing to have happened to him. He'd been so happy that his other brothers had met theirs that he'd been taking mental notes on what to do and not to do when she came along. Ivan wasn't even worried about his house being right for her. All the other women were just fine with whatever had been done to the houses when they moved in. He could expect no less from his mate.

Now that he had his clinic to work at, he was excited to see what she might be adding to the family. And the other women had added more to the family even if it was their personalities. And each one of them had their own kind of personality to add to any gathering, too.

By two in the afternoon, the snow had stopped

and the roads were cleared. He took his time driving home and was glad when he got there. The roads were kind of slick in places, and he was thankful when he was able to pull into his own garage for the rest of the day. He wasn't even going out for milk if he didn't have any.

~*~

"Sen, you have a phone call. What have I told you about getting phone calls at work?" She said nothing because she'd never gotten one before. "Oh well, don't do it again. It takes up too much of my time to try to find you."

"I'm right here in the office next to yours, Ben. Just chill." She was working on a project that would get more feet in the mall, which would mean a healthy way to impact the little town she lived in. Turning the now-defunct mall into something better had been a project that she'd been given six weeks ago, and she was having fun with it. "This is Serenity Bash. How can I help you?"

"Sen? Is that you?" Her mother. Just what she didn't need right now. "They've taken your uncle off life support, and he died." She made it sound as if it had been a big inconvenience for her to have been the one to tell her that her only uncle had passed away.

"When was he in the hospital?" Mom told her not to be dragging shit up that she didn't have any answers to. "Mom. He's obviously been in the hospital for some time now. When did you know that he was that sick? And why didn't you call me?"

"It happened about two weeks ago. They said that he had a stroke and that he might not make it. I got tired of being in here with him every day, so I asked them to take life support off him, and they finally did it today. He didn't last any longer than the machine being stopped before he stopped breathing. What's the big deal?"

"I'm surprised that you even bothered to call me since it's not a big deal. He was my only uncle and your only brother, so you should have called me when he had the stroke." She could almost see her mom waving her off like she was asking too much of her. "Where's Aunt Cindy? Shouldn't she have been a part of the life support questions?"

"She died too." Sen would have hung up on her mother if she weren't worried that she'd never get any information other than what she had now. "The car accident that he caused by having a stroke killed her, too. She didn't even make it to the hospital. They're waiting on the thing with your uncle before I have to make funeral arrangements for both of them. I wish now that I'd have called you. I'm going to have to do this on my own, I think. Unless you want to do it. I'd be happy to turn it all over to you if you will do it right."

"I'm pretty sure that they're arrangements have been made. Uncle Robert was good about getting things settled before it was time to use them. I don't suppose you've done anything about your prearrangement, have you?" She said she had plenty of time. "Sure, and I'm sure that Uncle Robert thought that, too, but he's prepared. Tell me where they are and I'll make arrangements to go there in the morning and talk to the funeral director."

After getting the information from her mom, she sat down at the desk in Ben's office and mourned the loss of her favorite two people in the world. Her mother wouldn't understand that, as she didn't like anyone but herself, and usually that was debatable. She decided to find the newspaper that was usually around and see what she could find out about the accident. Surely there would be something more than what she'd gotten from her mother about it.

After finding the newspaper that she wanted, Sen wasted no time in getting to reading it. It had been two weeks ago like her mom had said, but Aunt Cindy had survived the accident only to die at the hospital a day later. Uncle Robert had had a stroke, they said, before he slammed into the car in front of them. Taking both cars up and into oncoming traffic, which killed just her aunt and uncle. The people in the other car had survived with only a few minor cuts and bruises.

Making a few more calls to the police department that had been in charge of the investigation, it was determined that her uncle was at fault even though there was little that could be done about his heart stroking out so she called a doctor friend of hers when she needed more information on the 'life support' that had been keeping her uncle alive for the last two weeks.

"It was a big one from what I've read about it. Even if he had been in the hospital with his body hooked up to monitors, he wouldn't have survived. Cindy was nearly decapitated. The reason it says that she died at the hospital a day later is that they were both donors and were kept alive because of their organs. Not everyone knows that. Your family was able to save six lives by being a donor, and made it so that four people will be able to see. More people should do that." She asked him what she needed to do now. "You're taking over for your mother? I hope the hell so. She'll fuck it up even if they do have their arrangements made."

"Yes, I'm taking over." She thought about what he said and wasn't even offended by what he said about her mom. She was a royal pain in the ass. "They do have their arrangements made, and everything should be paid for. Whatever is left over will go to their estate. Whatever that might entail."

Her aunt and uncle were good people, and

while she had no idea what their estate might be, she knew that they lived modestly and didn't seem to have trouble paying for things when they came up. She was going to miss them both terribly.

Finishing up what she'd been working on, Ben allowed her to leave to take care of things for them. Once she was at the funeral directors, she was told that everything was indeed paid for and that all the arrangements had been made. She was glad for that. It made the whole process seem more personal to her, rather than her having to guess what they might want done.

She did decide for them to have services together and for there to be one room used for the two of them. Sen knew they were well-liked and thought of, so she didn't have any trouble agreeing to the one full day of calling hours with the service the next day. Everything else had been taken care of by them.

After getting things arranged, she made her way to the police station, where she got an update on the accident. It was just as she'd been told. Uncle Robert had had a stroke, causing the accident that pushed traffic at a light, killing her aunt immediately. Her uncle, brain-dead from the stroke, was kept alive so that his organs could be harvested, as he and his wife had been donors forever.

Going back to her apartment, she was surprised

to find a box from someone on her doorstep. Taking it inside, she was dismayed to find her mother waiting for her in her living room. She asked her what she was doing.

"That landlord of yours wasn't going to allow me to come in until I told him about Robert. I had to lie and tell him that you knew I was meeting you here so he'd allow me in. Why do you lock your door anyway, Sen? It's not like you have anything worth stealing. Besides, it makes it difficult for me to get into your place when you're not home." She told her that was the point of the lock. "I don't understand. You want me to be locked out of your place? Whyever for? I'm your mother. As I said, you have nothing that anyone wants anyway. How did the arrangements go?"

"Well, they were all done up like I knew that they would be. I only had to approve the calling hours for them." She picked up her mom's boots and put them by the door. "The next time you break into my place, could you at the very least clean up after yourself? I might not have anything to steal, but I do like the things that I have."

"Oh, get over it." Her mom put her feet up on the couch, and Sen was happy that at least she didn't have her muddy boots on. "I've come here to stay until the will is read. I'm sure he had one. Since he outlived Cindy, if there isn't a will, it will all come to me. I've never cared for her in the first place. Not good enough for my big brother."

"I loved her, and she was good enough for Uncle Robert. They were a great couple." Mom did that waving her off thing again, and it annoyed her. "Use your words, Mom. I know you have plenty of them. You never seem to run out when you're talking to me."

"You're in a mood." She said that her favorite uncle and aunt had died. "They were old, darling, and they were going to die anyway. Why don't you take me shopping, and we'll get some lunch? Well, it's too late for lunch, so we'll have an early dinner. Your treat."

"I don't want to have an early dinner with you, and I can't afford to go shopping with you. In fact, I can't afford dinner with you either. You always pick the most expensive places when it's my 'treat'. On top of that, you usually want to have your nails done or something along those lines, and I don't have the money for it." She asked why she was forever broke. Telling her that she was going to have to manage her money better. "I do, but when you come around, I have to pick eating peanut butter sandwiches for the rest of the week or my rent. I decided that telling you *no* is better on my wallet and stomach."

Even though she said she was going to stay, her mom left about an hour later. She left her with a migraine as well as an upset belly. Taking something for both, Sen laid down on her cleaned up couch and closed her eyes. It was easier to deal with her ailments than with her mother staying the night when she wasn't really invited. She was going to have to talk to the landlord about him letting her mom into her place, too. Mom was the main reason that she had locks on her door in the first place.

Chapter 9

Guy sat in his office trying to figure out where he wanted to go next. He'd been sitting in here for the last two hours, and all he could think about was that Amber wasn't home and he was bored. He never got bored when he was alone in the house, and he couldn't figure out why it was suddenly bothering him now.

"Because you've opened up your heart and now they all want in it for some reason." He had opened his mind too; he didn't snap anymore, nor did he enjoy his own company. He was blaming that on his family. They had pushed and shoved their way into his head and heart, and now they were there all the time. "Stupid family."

Smiling, he thought about what Belinda would have said about that statement. She would have yelled at him and told him that the best thing in the world was family and that he should appreciate them more. Guy had gotten in the habit of talking to himself because he wanted Belinda to hear him and shake him out of his mood. But she was gone now, and he missed the dead woman.

No other ghosts had come around him. He could see them. Not as many as Selma did, but he could see them hanging out in places. More than likely, they didn't understand that he could see them standing about. It was just as well; he didn't want anything to do with them any more than they did him.

Just this morning, one showed up in his office. Ignoring them in favor of looking things up for the coming spring, he decided that if they didn't bother with him, then he'd be all right not to be bothered by them. It was a win-win situation for him. Not so much for the ghosts, he supposed.

He had enough going on right now with deadlines for upcoming books as well as things around the house being done, so that when the spring auctions came along, he'd know just what he needed in the way of the household. They needed bedroom suits for sure, and if he could find a couple of landscape pictures to go into the rooms, he'd be thrilled about that.

There were other things that he thought would fill out the rooms. Objects of curiosity would be nice, along with a few rugs in the right price range, as all the rooms had hardwood floors. He and Amber discussed it, and they wanted to name the rooms by color. Having it called the blue room or the yellow room would also make it easier to have guests put in specially named rooms rather than saying the one at the top of the stairs. It was something that he was looking forward to a great deal.

He looked up from his now sleeping computer to see what Amber wanted when she called his name. Her smile could mean anything, but he waited for her to tell him what she needed. She came further into the room while he waited for her to speak.

"I just spoke to Ivan again. He wants to know if you want to go with him to an auction that is set up in one of the bigger buildings in Zanesville. He said it's an open affair and that means that there might be more than one lot at the auction." He asked when it was. "Tomorrow morning. He said it's one of his favorite auctioneers who is running it, and he wants us both to go with him. I think the clinic is closed on Thursdays."

"It is, and what do you think about going? It won't be like a house auction, but it could be fun. And it will get us out of the house. I'm sort of bored with the same walls. How about you?" She said she was game if he was. "Good. Tell him that—I'll tell him we'll go. We'll take the truck if the weather holds. Do you know what it's supposed to do tomorrow?"

"Sunny all morning and into the afternoon. Then storm clouds build up after seven for it to drop another inch or two of the wet stuff on us." She laughed. "I'm not normally so up on the weather channel, but I was just in the kitchen and Katy was saying how she needs to go to the grocery store tomorrow on her day off."

"Good. We'll go." He rubbed his hands together. "You get the name of the building, and I'll check to see if it has heat or not. More than likely it does, but just how much heat will be the question. I went to one once, and the heat was all right, but the floor seemed to be doubly cold, and my legs and feet ached when I walked around. I don't know if the concrete was just too cold or if I'd strained something the day before. But we'll be prepared."

By the time he got in touch with his brother, it was late in the day. He'd gotten a little more work done, an outline for the next detective book, and was working on a title when he remembered that he needed to contact his brother. Armed with the name of the building and the way it was going to be heated, he figured they'd be all right when the time came for them to be hanging out at the auction house. Both he and his wolf couldn't stand to be cold, unlike his brothers, who loved to romp in the snowy weather like big wolves did.

Going up to bed later that night, he was very happy to see that Amber was naked. She mostly wore one of his shirts to sleep in, but when she was in the mood, she was as naked as the day she was born. He got into the bed just as unclothed as she was.

"What did you have in mind tonight?" Guy

wiggled his brows at her, causing her to laugh. "We could make love, and I'd love that. I've been chasing you around the house for days now, and it's been fun, but I'd like to have you in the bed beneath me."

"That's what I need too. Comfort sex." He didn't know what that meant, but he'd give her anything she wanted if he could. Pulling her into his arms as soon as the sheets between them were gone, he kissed her fully on the mouth and leaned back to look down at her. "It's been a long day. A longer week, it seems to me."

He'd forgotten that she made arrangements for her brother and sister to be cremated today. Neither of them had a will, and so she made their arrangements as next of kin. Their estate, what very little of it there was, would be sold off, and the money that came from the sale would be used to pay for their funeral and services that had been incurred.

Touching her as gently as he could, Guy loved the little sounds that she made when he did so. Her flesh was so warm that he found himself wanting to kiss her everywhere he exposed with his hands. Getting to her breasts, he took the large tip into his mouth and suckled just on her nipple. Her hand in his hair was all the sign that he needed that she was enjoying herself. Moving beyond her breasts, he nibbled on her ribs and around to her back when he touched her. Rolling her to her front, he licked her down her spine to the two dimples that were on either side of her. Lifting her up and sitting her on his lap when he rolled to his back again, he looked up at her.

"Set the pace for us, love. Ride me as you wish." Her hips moved slowly at first, and he put his hands on her hips. When she needed steadying, he did so with just a small squeeze to her thighs. Reaching up, he filled his hands with her beautiful breasts and then sat up enough to take them into his mouth at the same time. She lost her rhythm in riding him for a moment, but she got right back into it when he kissed her again. "You're beautiful. I love you."

"I love you as well, Guy. So much. But I need to come." In due time, he told her and helped her out by slowing her down again and again. "Please. I need to come. Come with me so that I can enjoy you even better."

Spreading his hands on her back, he tried to slow her down even more. Finally, when she had had enough of his help, she rolled them to the bed where she was beneath him. With her legs wrapped around his hips, she continued the rolling of her hips until he needed to come with her. She was a sneaky little minx.

So that he did have some control over their lovemaking, he took her hands to the head of the bed. Holding her there with one of his hands, he explored the rest of her body by running his hands up her rib cage to her breasts to her hips. He could tell when she was getting closer than before. Still holding her hand above them, he fucked her a little harder when he entered her and watched her face. She had the most expressive face when they were making love that he nearly forgot what he was doing when she ground her hips into his groin.

"You're not terribly nice when you want something, are you?" She said he was taking too long. "I could let you come now and then me later after I've had my fill of you."

"No, you have to come with me. I love it when you fill me while I'm coming. It's like we're two stars colliding in the sky when that happens." He felt his cock stretch within her. "That's it, Guy. Give me more of yourself. Give me your all so that I can see the stars. I need to see them with you."

His own rhythm was temporarily stopped when she ground her hips into him again. It was like she was begging for him to release, and he wanted to make it last. When she dug her nails into his shoulders, it was as if his wolf roared at him to take her. Guy pulled her ass up to meet each of his downward strokes until she came screaming out his name. For a few seconds, no more, he didn't feel anything. Nor could he hear anything. Then, as if a switch had been turned on, he came hard, fucking her through two more heady climaxes before he fell atop her in dizziness.

Guy felt the bed move around, not in the room but with her moving to get out from beneath him. He wanted to help, move off her, but it seemed to be too much effort, and he just didn't have it in him to move anymore. Finally, when she settled down, he was covered up by the blankets. He rolled his head to the side and looked at his lovely mate.

"Did I hurt you?" She smiled at him and told him he was using too many words. "All right. I'm exhausted now, thanks to you, so I'm going to sleep."

He thought even before he finished speaking that he was out. His mind and body simply saying enough was enough, and he slept hard. He hoped the house never caught fire; he'd be one dead wolf if it did.

At four, he woke up needing to use the bathroom. He debated whether or not he'd make it or fall on his face, but almost as soon as he got up, he knew that he should have had a cane or something to get him there and back. Once he was back in bed, he fell asleep again once the blankets were over him.

Just as the sun was coming up, he had to get up again. It wasn't like him to get up more than once in the middle of the night to go to the bathroom, but once he got there this time, he knew that he was up for the day and decided to take a shower. Being as quiet as he could, he was dressed and out of the room just as the sun was cresting the mountains behind their home. Breakfast was next on his list of things to get done while up so early.

Making pancakes had never been something that he was good at. He could do it, but they were never round, nor did they look done on one side. Usually, he ended up burning the first batch as he'd get easily sidetracked, but when the cook came in and took over, he was glad to see that she didn't dump out his mixture in favor of her own. He liked his cinnamon pancakes more when they had apple chunks in them. And he loved the apple flavor in pancakes. Amber came down just as he was getting his second plate full.

"You should have woken me up. I want to go today too." He'd forgotten about the auction and told her that. "I should have set an alarm; I knew we had to get up early."

"Ivan said he'd be here around nine. It's only twenty minutes away to the hall that they're using. Dress in layers so that when it gets warmer outside, we won't roast too much." She said she was wearing extra socks so her feet didn't get cold. "Me too. I can be cold everywhere else, but not my feet. When they're cold, I'm cold all over."

They were both waiting for Ivan when he showed up. Taking their advice, he had worn double the socks, too. But he had on layers of a t-shirt, sweatshirt, and then a jacket, so that he could peel things off when it got warmer. You know it's been cold, he thought when thinking forty degrees was a heatwave outside. But spring was just a month away, so they didn't have much longer to wait for it to stay warmer outside. Or not. You never knew what the weather was going to be like from day to day in Ohio.

The three of them had fun on the way over. Since they were going to use his truck, he drove. Ivan sat up front with him, and Amber sat in the back, making it possible to hear one another when they spoke. Finding a great parking space, they were in line to get their numbers in no time.

The day started out with glassware. He'd never been a fan of it himself, but Amber saw a couple of pieces that she thought would go perfect in the blue bedroom. He stood with her when she bid and was happy that she didn't get caught up in the moment. Leaving her to it, he and his brother walked around the furniture. There was a great deal of it in here today, when normally it was tools that were in abundance.

Since he knew measurements, he was able to figure out which bedroom suite he wanted and which ones didn't fit in the room. A queen would be great in the room, he knew, but a king would be better. A single bed wouldn't work at all, but he did notice that there was a set of bunk beds that were of good quality. He and Ivan looked them over while they were auctioning off the tables and chairs that were in the lots.

Once they got a good look at the bunk beds, they could tell that it wasn't worth ten bucks. The only thing that it would be good for was the wood, and since he didn't want to haul it home and take care of it, they decided not to bid on it. Sometimes things looked good until they didn't. That was the one and only thing that his father had taught him.

Amber won what she wanted in that she got some glass pieces for the blue bedroom they were going to be working on, and some things in the prettiest shade of yellow he'd ever seen for the room of the same name. Since she was having such a good time, he told her about the bunk beds, and she was happy that they'd looked at it. Now it was time for the bedroom suites. Ivan wanted two of them, and they were going to try to get the rest. That would be a total of eight bedroom suites for him to take home in his truck. Laughing, he said he was glad it was so close to home; they would need to make several trips.

By the end of the afternoon, they were able to get all but one of the bed sets. He was thrilled with their purchases, and Amber got some other things for the rest of the rooms. They were looking at rugs when his brothers joined them to load up the furniture that they'd already gotten. It was going to look like they were moving out again by the amount of help they had.

The rugs were the last of the items that they were bidding on, and he was happy that Amber was able to get the auctioneer to roll out the rugs so she could see the colors. There was only the one that they wanted, and it seemed that it was going to go into the yellow room. The motif was a beautiful pattern of muted colors of yellow and brown that he really liked. They were going to get one more to put in the laundry room so that the floor wouldn't seem so hard.

Not only did they get both rugs, but since the auctioneer couldn't get anyone else to bid on them, he gave them to Amber. She asked Ivan if he wanted any of them, and he took the rest. His rooms didn't have carpet in them either, and he'd need something soft and warm to put on the floor so when you got up in the morning, you wouldn't have frozen feet.

The blue bedroom was finished, but for the mattress, box springs, and linens. They'd been looking at a set online that they liked and were glad that it measured out to be a queen-sized bed. The other beds were all kings, and he loved that even more.

Ivan decided that he wanted subs for dinner; it was quick and easy, he said, and they joined him. Katy fried them some potatoes to go with them, and they were set. It wasn't long after getting the beds set up that they were all ready for bed. Ivan almost stayed again, but he needed to get to the clinic first thing, and he wanted a shower. That was fine by him, he wanted to look around his nicely finished up bedrooms.

~*~

The day had started out fine for walking, but it soon turned to shit. Getting to her family's home, she decided that she was going to drive everywhere until the weather turned nice for good. That could be forever, she knew, but she was sick of having wet clothing when the snow fell on her from the trees.

"The house will need to be emptied out." She never cared for this woman, but she'd been assigned to help her finish with the estate of her brother and sister. If she didn't cool her jets, she was going to call the attorney's office and have her taken off the case. She had better things to do than to be badgered like she was all the time. "The whole house is a mess." Amber had had enough.

"I'm aware of that. I didn't live here, but my dead brother and sister did, who I just laid to rest yesterday. Will you please just back off until I get my bearings? I'm tired of you acting like it all has to be perfect for you. If it were perfect, I'd not need your skinny ass helping." The look on the other woman's face was perfect, and she was glad that she stood up for herself. "I know that the house is a mess. That's what you're here for: to tell me what has to be gone or sold with the house."

"I'd empty it out and hope for a good buyer with a blind eye for décor." Her little bit of laughter was all that saved her from being kicked out on her ass. "It looks like it's all outdated, including the kitchen. You'll be lucky if you get what they paid for it."

"They inherited it like I did my home." She looked around the kitchen and decided that in order to sell it at all, something was going to have to be done to the place. Not only the kitchen, and it was the worst, but the carpets throughout the house were as old as she was, she mused, and there was still a house phone in the place. Yes, it would need to be updated before she could get a good price for it.

"I've only just decided to have it remodeled. Just looking at this floor makes me realize that no one was going to purchase it at this price. I grew up in this home, so I know that it's as old as that, so I won't need your help after all. Tell your boss I'm sorry." She actually huffed at her. "You need to find a way to be less offensive, lady, before someone takes you to task. I have better things to do with my time than to spend it with a huffing, puffing woman who thinks she knows it all."

On that note, she turned and left her standing in the middle of the most run-down room in the house, the living room. Even the shag carpet was worn in places. How they were excited about living here was beyond her, but then they didn't pay anything for it, and that could be it. She went back to the house to get her car, as she had to go into town again and order mattresses for the bedrooms.

It was nearly noon when she made her way back home. She'd spoken to the attorney's office twice about the remodel of the house, and they were going to secure her a loan against the house for her to do it with. When speaking to Devlin, he told her not to go that way; they would want a say in what's done or not, and that Brandy said she'd loan her the money until the sale of the house went through. She liked that idea much better.

Ticking things off her list, she was nearly done with it when she ended up at the grocery store. She just wanted one of those cups of fruit they sold so that she'd make it to dinner. After getting just the one that she wanted, she sat in her warm car and ate it. The bits of watermelon were all right, but the other fruit made her think of summer and warmer weather. She needed that as soon as it could come. Picking up her cell when it rang, she saw that it was Guy.

"Hello, big guy. Did you ever get made fun of because of your name being Guy? That just occurred to me." He laughed and told her that only on occasion did he get teased, but since he played football, they mostly called him Fraizer. "What can I do for you?"

"My publisher and good friend has talked me into doing a book signing. I've never done one before, but with you by my side, I think I could do it. The only issue is that it's in Florida. What do you think about traveling to Florida this time next month and hanging out with me at a book convention?" She asked him if he was serious. "I am. I was a lot meaner when I started writing, and he said that I would really bring a lot of people to the event for the lesser-known writers. I'm not so sure how many will actually come to see me, but I told him that if you agreed to go with me, I'd do it. So what do you say?"

"I think it sounds fun. I've actually been to a book signing once. It was a great deal of fun to meet the people behind your favorite books. It's been a while, but I'm sure not much has changed. Yes, I'd love to go with you."

"Good. We'll fly down and back. The convention is for five days. They wanted me to be the guest speaker at this late notice, but I said I'd rather just be in and question and answer thing this first time. I wouldn't know what to say to a bunch of people, but he said I'd do fine." She said she had all the confidence in the world in him. "I'm glad you do. And I knew that you would too. You're my hero, did I tell you that?"

"No, but I don't know about all of that. I just love you, that's all." He said that he loved her as well. "I have most of my list done now, so I'll be heading home soon. Do you know when you'll be back?"

"Late. After the meeting with my publisher about some issues with the editor, I'm going to meet a group of them to see what I can do about getting my books out safer. There are all kinds of places stealing my work and putting it up on free links. I don't know what can be done about that, but I know that it's an issue." She told him that she'd read about it too and that it hurts every author who has them on the free sites. "I don't know if people realize how much they're hurting authors when they get them from that site. It's like taking money out of our pockets."

After talking about the illegal downloading of books, they talked about her list. She was able to mark one more thing off the list: what to have for dinner when he said that he wanted comfort food. She knew just what he wanted in food like that and told him she'd talk to Katy when she got home. Making lists had always been something that she loved doing, especially when she could mark things off from them like she was able to do today.

When she was driving again, this time headed to the post office to pick up several boxes that had been delivered there instead of at home, she noticed that the snow was melting off at a good rate. Not that she didn't care for the white fluffy stuff, it was beautiful at the holidays, she was just tired of it and wanted the green grass and flowers to come around.

She was just pulling into the driveway when Brandy called her. She wanted her to meet her at the house with her foreman. She loved that the woman liked to get things done quickly, but in honesty, she just wanted to go home, kick off her shoes, and take a nap. But duty called, and she made her way to her brother's home instead.

"It's a mess, isn't it? Did they have help?" She told her that she didn't think that they could have afforded it and left it at that. "I can have someone clean it out for you and sell off the things that are in here. The fridge can go and the stove. When you remodel, you'll need to update those as well."

"I just want it finished, but be honest. If it takes a year to do that, then that's all right too. Do you understand?" She said that she did and told her that she'd take care of it for her. "Thank you, but you don't have to do that. They were my brother and sister. Did I tell you that they're still going to be convicted of murder? It has to be done so that I can get any money from the estate after I sell everything off. There wasn't much. Just this old house and a few things that they had that were theirs in here."

"If they find any insurance later, you can get that as well." She nodded, not wanting to be in the house any longer than she had to. "So what sort of kitchen did you want? The rest of the house will be easy. Just do the walls, and I'm assuming pull up all the carpet."

"Yes, for sure on the carpet. And in order to make the kitchen right, I think you should ask a cook. I wouldn't know the first thing about redoing a kitchen, but someone who might cook in the house might. The house is big enough for a staff for sure. We can use yours or mine; it matters little to me." She looked around the room. "They didn't even have a coffee pot or one of those pod things, did they? I know they drank coffee. I suppose that's where they lost a lot of money, not being able to brew them a cup of it when they wanted it."

"There are other things missing as well. Did you notice that while the fridge is old, there isn't an ice maker? They had a bag of ice on top of the ice trays, and even those are old." She and Brandy laughed about the lack of everyday things. Like, there wasn't even a microwave in the room. Much less something like a popcorn popper. "I wonder how they had even a snack in the evening without anything to cook or pop it in?"

Walking through the rest of the house, she was glad to be doing this with Brandy. She made it fun, and the decisions to get rid of things were easier with her. As soon as they finished the tour of the house, she felt a good deal better about the entire renovation of the house, instead of just putting it off too long. She was glad that they were such good friends, too.

Chapter 10

Devlin didn't so much as take a sip of his tea, not wanting to bring attention to himself and the thought of getting wrapped up in their—he thought they were mother and daughter—drama was simply going to ruin his day, and he didn't want that to happen. He was here to help a client with the death of her family, and he didn't even want to do that.

"You said that I could help you." The daughter, he could see the resemblance now, said she'd not said that and that she didn't want or need her help; it was all arranged. "You're just wanting to make sure you're in the will. I know how you are. You're nothing but selfish, Sen, nothing but a selfish daughter who never looks out for her mother."

"If that were true, then how do you suppose I made sure that you had a winter coat for this trip here? Or the boots you have on? Not to mention the handbag that you just had to have right now when things are tight for me." Her mother waved her off, and that seemed to piss the girl off again. "Mom, I have this. There isn't any need for you to help when Uncle Robert had everything planned out to the minute. They'll have calling hours, then that will be it until the burial. After that, that's when the will needs to be read."

"Then why do you need an attorney?" She said that the other office, the one reading the will, said she should bring one. "Well, I want one too. Or better yet, we'll share yours. That way, I don't have to have you find me one when the reading is in four days."

"You get your own. He told me that I would need one, not that we should share one. If you think you need someone to go with you, then I suggest that over the next few days, you find someone. I'm washing my hands of you." She asked her daughter what that meant. "It means I'm not sharing my attorney, nor am I getting you one. If you need one, which I have no reason to believe you do since you weren't told to get one, then I'm finished with this conversation."

"Selfish. That's what you are is selfish. I didn't raise you to be this way." She pointed out that she was raised by nannies and not by her in the first place. "Yes, and look what that got me. A selfish daughter who never learned how to share. I shouldn't have allowed my brother to but in when you were little. I should have raised you myself."

"I think I'm well adjusted for someone who had a mother like you." That seemed to be true, he thought, since the older woman didn't understand shit. "Now hush. I'm supposed to be meeting Mr. Fraizer here any moment."

"I'm here." She smiled at him, but he could tell that she was embarrassed. And he was as well. "I didn't mean to eavesdrop on your conversation, but you were too into it before you came in here." He stood up and towered over both women and felt good when the older woman backed up. He didn't use his height for intimidation often, but today it felt justified. "I believe that our table is ready, Ms. Ranger."

It was only a two-top and no room for the other woman. But she pulled a chair from another table and tried her best to shove her way into it. The manager of the restaurant had to be called, and they were put at a four-top with a lot of room for him to spread out. Devlin wasn't going to deal with the mother and her temper tantrum. He let Ms. Ranger deal with her mom. She seemed to be good at it.

After going over the menu, he decided on a nice salad. He didn't want to eat anything like a burger, where he might get something on his tie or suit. Instead of having iced tea, however, he did have some soda. It was something that he rarely treated himself to, and today seemed like a good day to have some.

"Is it all right with you if we don't discuss the will reading until after we eat? I'm fearful of getting indigestion, and I think my mom will get bored if we put it off and leave." She looked pointedly at her mom. "I don't know why you have to barge into this with me. You didn't even care for your brother, and you certainly had no love for his wife. Why do you care anyway what the will says? It's doubtful that he had much for anyone to leave behind. He was a great man, and I love my aunt, but rich they were not."

"I was told I was left something and I'm going to be there to get it." Ms. Ranger said to suit herself, and after ordering, he could tell that the mother was getting bored with the light conversation that the two of them were having. "What kind of attorney are you anyway?"

"I work for my family for the most part. And Judge Rainer asked me to go over this with Sen so that she wasn't caught unaware." She asked what that meant. "I'm not sure. He just asked if I'd do him a favor and sit with his favorite clerk, and I said I'd do it. Usually, I just read over contracts and the likes for my family, as I said."

"So you're not much of an attorney then." He let her ramble on about his lack of skills until his lunch was brought. He noticed that she'd ordered a salad too, but it was the kind that had all kinds of add-ons with it, like chicken and cheese. His opinion was that if you wanted a salad, why mess it up with all kinds of extras and not just eat the greens? But it wasn't up to him today, so he kept his mouth shut. "I don't know why you came here; they never have the dressing that I like. Why don't they carry the house dressing at the pizza place that I like? That would be good if all restaurants carried the same dressing, don't you think?"

"I think it would no longer be the house dressing if everyone carried it, Mom. Just eat what you want and be done with it." They talked about the weather and how it was a lovely, almost spring-like day. He was telling them about how his brother and his wife were remodeling their home when Mrs. Ranger got bored and tried to liven up the conversation by talking about how her brother had done her dirty on more than one occasion. Neither he nor the younger woman commented, but let her ramble on about things that seemed to him would be better held in a private setting. She really didn't care for her brother.

Just as Sen, as he'd been asked to call her, said, her mother was bored and decided that she was going to go shopping. When she asked Sen for her credit card, he thought that they were going to get into another fight, but Sen held her ground, and her mother huffed off with her new handbag at her side and nothing more.

After their plates were cleared away, he got down to business. He didn't mind waiting until they were finished; in fact, he did the same thing with his family, eating first, then talking about things afterwards. He didn't feel rushed and put out either. It was a nice feeling.

"Did Judge Rainer give you any indication as to why I'd need an attorney? I mean, as much as I'm pissed at my mother, he didn't tell her to bring one with her." Instead of answering, he asked her how much she knew about her uncle and aunt. "They were very good people. They paid for me to go to private school. But when I was little, they paid for a nanny too. Said my mom was too busy with her projects to raise me properly. I never knew what projects they were talking about, but I didn't care. I had a wonderful childhood because of them."

"Could there have been a great deal of money?" She told him that they lived in a little two-bedroom home that was forever being repaired. When asked why they didn't move, she didn't know an answer. "He didn't give me any indication as to why he thought you'd need an attorney with you, but I don't mind going with you. I like Judge Rainer and always have. He's been a good mentor to me since I was in one of his classes in college."

"He said that he'd rather I was prepared than not. I have no idea why he'd think I need that. Unless it was to hold me up when I get sick of my mom. She can be a handful when she gets something in her head." He didn't say anything, but he believed her. "What will you do for me if there is something like a lot of money? I can't imagine that the house is worth all that much. I've not been to it in a few years. For all I know, they might well have gotten it looking really nice and are leaving it to me. That would be great. I hate living in an apartment."

"If there is a great deal of money or even a little, I can advise you on how you should spend it and see if there are any estates that go with it. There could be another house or something along those lines." He thought of something else. "As you said, he could have left you the house, and that would take some attorney work to get it in your name and the deeds as well. It sounds like, from what you're saying, that even if the estate is small, you'll need guidance on what to do to make it your own. What will your mother have to say if you get the house? Will she be upset?"

"She's upset about everything that has to do with Uncle Robert and especially my aunt Cindy. She's misremembering what my childhood was like and taking credit for the way I turned out. If not for the help of my uncle and aunt, I might well have been just like my mom and critical of everything." She looked away before speaking again. "I sometimes wonder why I was never liked by my mom. She's been nothing but mean to me since I can remember. My dad was never in the picture, so I'm glad that I had my uncle around all the time. He was a great influence on me when I was growing up."

After getting things squared away with Sen, he made his way home, telling her that he had a few more things to look into about the estate. He wasn't going to do a background check like he might well have done beforehand, but told her that he'd take her advice on the couple and they'd go from there. Whatever happened, it was going to be a good thing, he predicted, and he was happiest for the young woman. He and Ivan were going to hang out tonight as the last of the Fraizer men that wasn't married and have a good time. He was to meet him at six at his house, and then they were going to go bar hopping from there. It was something that neither of them did, and they were going to enjoy it as much as they could.

"You smell weird." He thanked his brother, then punched him in the shoulder. "I'm not kidding. You smell like...well, I was going to say sunshine, but we've not had much of that lately, so I wouldn't know." He said that he'd had lunch with a young woman today. Maybe that was it. "You were dressed like you are now? Not too professional of you, now, is it?"

They both laughed, and he told his brother that he'd worn a suit, so that couldn't be right. After a few more minutes of teasing him, Ivan seemed to have had enough and changed the subject. He was glad; he didn't want to be pissed off at his brother before they were out the door. Instead, he told him of the puppy he'd seen today.

"Usually I don't get to see just one puppy, but a whole litter. This little guy looked to be a bit of everything. But the little boy who had him assured me that he was going to be a little dog. However, I know better. Whatever the boy said, he had paws big enough to hold onto a basketball if he was so inclined." Devlin asked him why the boy thought it was going to be small. "His mom said he couldn't have a big dog. I was worried about that when he told me. What would she do if the dog were big, but she seemed all right when I pointed out that he had huge paws. She either didn't know the old saying or she didn't care. Whichever it was, I hope they have plenty of money for dog food."

They were on their second bar when they both decided that this whole thing wasn't what they wanted to do. Getting into a pizza shop that sold beers, the two of them shared two large pizzas along with the salad bar and sat around and talked. The place wasn't all that busy for a Friday night, so they didn't feel bad for taking up a table that could have been turned over to others coming in.

"Did you hear about Guy and Amber's home? They have it finished up, and it looks great. I don't think that it's going to be hard for them to have guests want to stay with them over Lica and Brandy's home. It's really nice." Ivan told him that he'd spent a couple of nights with them, too, when the weather was bad. "Then you've met their cook? She can cook for me if I thought that I could steal her away from them. Her blueberry lemon loaf is to die for. And she has just enough icing on it to make you drool."

They both had houses thanks to Brandy having money for it, but they didn't neither of them care for their home. Ivan liked his a little better than he did, but he wished he'd gone bigger rather than smaller when he'd been looking. The bigger houses seemed to suit his brother, and that was the route that he wished he'd taken. They both regretted buying the first one that they came across.

"Did I tell you that I ordered myself a new Jeep? It's one of the larger ones that I've wanted since I learned to drive. It's supposed to be coming in next week. I got it without all the bells and whistles on it and spent the money having it with nice seats rather than the cloth ones that it usually had on it." Ivan congratulated him. "Thanks. This one has four-wheel drive, which I'm looking forward to. I told you that I got stuck in the snow three times this year so far. I love the cold, but not when I have to drive in it."

Ivan had purchased his clinic from the man who

had been vet before. It was a nice little place, but it had a great list of clientele. Not that anybody who met Ivan didn't like him immediately, but it was nice having a practice where you were busy all the time and had a built-in client list. He had started out on his own with his practice, but he'd had Brandy's help. And with the way things were going for her and Lica, he'd never be out of work for two of them. They had billions of dollars and more businesses around the world than anyone he'd ever met before.

When the pizza place closed up, they left too. It was still early, only ten o'clock, and they weren't finished hanging out together. So instead of finding them another bar, which they didn't want to do, the two of them ended up at Devlin's place to watch some television and have a good night. And if they ended up staying in the same house for the night, that was fine too. The two of them were as close as brothers could get.

They talked about the upcoming reading of the will and how the mother of the woman was a fruitcake. Then he changed that to mean that she was just too critical about everything. He told Ivan about the salad that she'd ordered.

"You know how I feel about salads." Ivan laughed and said that everyone knew about his salad preferences. "She orders a salad and tells the waiter that she doesn't want yellow cheese on it and that they have to take out the croutons. Then she lists off other things that she doesn't want in her salad, like cucumbers, onions, and spinach. That's practically the whole thing. She might well have been better off ordering just a lettuce salad and been done with it. But she had him repeat it back to her three times, what she wanted out of it. And here I am waiting for my turn to order just a chef salad without any changes. I think that I wouldn't have had any changes for the man by the time she was finished, even if I had to pick things out for myself." They both laughed. "Then she wants things in it, like asparagus and scallops. I'm glad she wasn't seated next to me when she got it. That does not sound like a good combination at all."

They talked about their days to each other. It was nice having someone to talk to all the time, and even when they weren't together, Devlin was forever making a mental list of things that he wanted to talk to Ivan about. They were the youngest of their parents and had suffered badly at their hands. Even now, there were scars on both of them, both mentally and physically, that they both wore, and it had shaped them into the men that they were.

Lica had gotten the worst from their parents when growing up because, for some reason, they hated him even more. When their mother had shot and killed their father, she'd wanted Lica to be the one to go to prison because she needed to be out to take care of the rest of them. Whatever that meant. But since the police were there when the shooting had taken place, they knew that she'd been lying when she told them that Lica had attacked and killed their father. To this day, she still says that it was all on him.

The six of them had grown up in an abusive home. It was brutal, really. For days on end, they'd be chained to the tree in their backyard without food or drink. Sometimes they'd have to get loose on their own rather than wait for them to remember they had children. If not for the Wilkins, they might have thought that all families were the same growing up. He surely did miss the two of them a great deal since he passed away, and Mrs. Wilkins had gone to live with her daughter a couple of states over.

By midnight, the two of them were yawning a great deal. Knowing that at least one of them had to get up early in the morning, they decided to get to bed. Sharing a room with Ivan wasn't that big of a deal. It had been the six of them sharing a single room when they were growing up, so this wasn't much different. In fact, it was kinda nice having someone like his brother so close.

~*~

Guy was deep into his writing when he saw something

move out of the corner of his eye. He didn't acknowledge the ghost standing there but continued what he'd been doing since he'd been interrupted. The man seemed to be looking at the items on his bookshelf and didn't turn when he started talking, presumably to himself.

"Used to have me a set of these when I was alive. I wonder which mongrel got them when I passed." He didn't seem to require an answer, so he let him continue to look at the nice chess set he'd gotten for Christmas from his brother Ayden. "Probably Paul. He always was the shiftiest of the lot."

Guy figured that the man was talking about his children. The other day, he'd had another woman come to his office, and she'd called her kids ingrates. He did wonder if anyone liked their children anymore and decided that it would be a good thing to think about when he and Amber had any. Would they be mongrels or ingrates?

As he wandered around the room, Guy finished up the chapter that he was on. It was going along well, the book, and he thought that in about a week, he'd be making notes on it. He had to do that so that he'd not have to read every book again after writing it. It was something that he knew a couple of authors did. He thought it would be difficult to do when you had a lot of books out there. He was happy for his seven, eight, counting the one that he was writing now.

"You ever talk to us?" He looked in the direction of the man before he could think that was a bad idea. "Yeah, I knew you were listening to me. I have something that I'd like for you to do for me. It's not against the law or anything. Just the request of a dead man to his kids."

"The mongrels, I'm assuming." He laughed. More like a cackling of a witch, but he didn't comment on it. "Before I agree, how did you know that you could come to me? I don't want a bunch of ghosties taking up all my time."

"Belinda said you did right by her and not to go blabbing it all around that you did. If you do. I've got me an issue that I need someone to take care of for me. I wasn't murdered like she was, but I have it in my head that one of the mongrels has done in their little sister. She's not so little anymore, I don't guess, but a woman. I've not seen her around for a few weeks. She usually goes to my grave and puts some pretty flowers on it, and I haven't seen hide nor hair of them flowers nor her. I'm fearful that someone killed her off."

"What's her name?" He pulled up his search engine to put her name in when the man, he should have gotten his name by now, started around the room. "Do you remember her name? Or yours for that matter?"

"What kind of fool do you take me for? Of

course, I know my name. I know hers, too. It's Carter. Carter Livingstone. She's about twenty-five now." Guy put it in the search line, and while it was gathering up the information, he asked the man his name. "William Livingstone. She's my great-granddaughter. Had a wonderful relationship with her when she was nothing but a spud growing up. But I knew she was going to amount to something even before she started hanging around me."

"The computer says that she's quite famous. An artist. Painter." He said that he knew all that. "It also says that she's had some tragic background in her life. Do you know what that means?"

"I died, didn't I?" He didn't know if that was what they were talking about until he got to the interview that she'd done recently. She said her grandda was a large part of her life. "She took it kinda hard when I passed away in my sleep. I should have had a few more years left with her, but my ticker decided something else."

"I'm sorry about that. Did you have heart problems before then?" He said that he'd been taking good care of himself for about the last two decades and didn't want to die so young. "You look to be in your late sixties, but I'm assuming that you're younger than that."

"I'm eighty-four. Turned that number a week

before I passed on. Birthdays still count with the dead, don't they?" Guy told him that he didn't know. Belinda had been the only ghost he'd encountered before him. "Well, we count them up like we're still around. I bet old Belinda could give you her age before and after she was murdered. Good woman that one. I wish I could have known about her before her getting killed by her mongrels."

"My wife is step-daughter to Belinda and half-sister to the mongrels. That's a good name for them, too." Shaking his head, he told him he was going to look him up, too. "If you're no better than your mongrel kids, I won't help you. I have enough things going on in my life."

Putting in the man's name, he was impressed that William had had a good life. And true to his word, he had been leading a good life up until he died. It also talked about the relationship he'd had with his granddaughter, Carter.

"She must have been a good girl." He did some more searches on the young woman and found that she traveled a great deal with her work, her art. He didn't want to do that, travel a great deal to promote his books. How would he get them done if he were forever out and about? "It says here that she traveled to Spain recently. Could she be on one of those trips right now, and maybe she didn't tell you? What reason would anyone have to hurt her? Do you have any idea?"

"She was my heir. Most of the mongrels didn't like that." He would assume not and told the elderly man that. "Left it all to her so that she could oversee my businesses and money. Quite a bit of that, too, I left her. But none to the mongrels. They took enough from me when I was around, forever with their hands out like I was some kind of bank or something. Not a one of them would work a job the way that my Carter did. She's got herself a good education, too. Them damned kids hurt her, I just know it."

"I'm looking here the best I can. But until I can talk to her boss or her attorney, then we don't want to assume the worst." He asked him if he thought it might kill him to be so stressed out all the time. "No, I didn't say that, but you thinking she's dead isn't going to get me moving any faster than I am. I have some leads that I can follow up on."

Guy had an entire notepad filled with information about Carter Livingstone before William said he was tired. That was something that he'd learned from Belinda about being around too much. It drained the dead. That was why she'd disappear for so long, so she could rest up some before coming back.

Making notes on what was going to be his investigative journey with the man, he also made notes of things that he was able to look up without knowing what he was looking for. It said that Carter had a publicist who would have her schedule, and that was where he was going to start. It might be a simple thing that she was on the road and nothing more. But for some reason, he didn't think so.

William also gave him the name of an attorney that she used, as well as his attorney. He had more with this mystery than he had with Belinda, but that didn't mean that it was going to be easier. He'd had to kill one of Belinda's mongrels, and that didn't even faze the other woman. She'd been murdered by them.

By the time he made his way up to bed, Amber having gone up hours ago, he had two pages of notes and a long list of things that he was going to do starting tomorrow. It didn't just list things that he was going to be doing for the Livingstone family, but a couple of things that he needed to get done for the house.

Even though it looked like it was finished, there were things that he needed to make sure were taken care of before he could deem it perfect. Amber had been in the bedrooms off and on for the last week and found that two of the windows were cracked and needed to be replaced. While he didn't think he'd know how to do that, he was going to make sure they were replaced.

He loved having his own home, something that as a kid he never dreamed possible. Or even obtainable.

But he had one now and thought that he'd never not want to be living in a house over living in an apartment or condo. There was just too much freedom in having a place of his own. And an added bonus was sharing with his mate, Amber, of course.

Before You Go...

HELP AN AUTHOR

write a review

THANK YOU!

Share your voice and help guide other readers to these wonderful books. Even if it's only a line or two your reviews help readers discover the author's books so they can continue creating stories that you'll love. Login to your favorite retailer and leave a review. Thank you.

AWARD WINNING, BESTSELLING AUTHOR

Kathi S. Barton is an award-winning and bestselling author known for her steamy paranormal romances and unforgettable characters. A recipient of the prestigious Pinnacle Book Achievement Award, her books have topped the charts on Amazon and All Romance eBooks, earning her a loyal global readership.

Kathi lives in Nashport, Ohio, with her husband, Paul. When she's not crafting passionate love stories set in magical worlds, she enjoys camping, exploring local auctions, and attending county fairs, where Paul showcases his artwork and pottery. Her creative spark—fueled by a muse she describes as a cross between Jimmy Stewart and Hugh Jackman—brings her stories to vivid, heartfelt life.

Paranormal romance with plenty of heat is her favorite genre, and she loves connecting with her readers. Feel free to reach out—Kathi would love to hear from you.

Email: aaronskiss@gmail.com

Blog: kathisbartonauthor.blogspot.com